BLOOD

FIERCELY

DEFENDED

BLOOD FIERCELY DEFENDED

HEATHER SPRAGUE

Many thanks to Dale for giving me the courage to pursue my passion at last.
Thanks also goes to Kristen, Glenna, Karen, Sabrina and Rosemary for your honest feedback. This novel would not be what it is without you.

CHAPTER 1

A face full of dragon fire hurts like a bitch. Anca put a fist on her hip and pointed a finger at the gray speckled dragon before her. "No fire at Derya!" The eighty-pound creature gave a small cough of flame. Anca could tell he wasn't happy. "Don't you sass me."

The dragon's long neck drooped in guilt.

"Go fish." Anca pointed to the gushing river not far away.

The dragon gave Anca one last look before leaping into the air over her head. He banked right to avoid a pine tree and landed on the bank of a gurgling river. He stared at it seriously for a moment before plunging his head into the icy depths and reemerging with a salmon in his jaws.

"I am so sorry," Derya said through her hands. Her expression almost made Anca forget that her face hurt, but not quite.

"He needs to learn not to play with you so rough yet." Anca's face was already starting to heal. Her skin stung as it loosened and morphed back to its usual caramel color.

"I'd heal," said Derya.

"Yeah, in a couple days, and your beautiful dark skin would have scars for almost a week. My scars will only last a day. Besides, you're my charge until you know this place well enough not to get trampled by an ogre."

Anca touched her long nose. The skin was beginning to smooth, another couple hours, and she'd just have some wicked scars. "And pay attention to where you walk in their section."

"The sod, right."

"It looks just like grass but will lead you exactly where you don't want to go."

"How do I avoid it?"

"This conservatory is designed to be like a mountain side, so it is best to stick to the rocks whenever you aren't sure where to put your feet. A geologist like yourself can tell us where we can add stone paths without messing with erosion or adversely affecting soil PH. levels."

She looked around in wonder. "I used to dig in my mother's garden as a child. I told her I was looking for unicorn bones. I never would have guessed how close I was to guessing the truth."

"We are pretty far underground. The subway system is fifty feet above the ceiling of this place.

Magick helps of course. Not card trick magic. Actual magick. The kind that bends light waves and levitates rocks," said Anca.

Derya nodded as she tucked her dusty pink hair out of her face. She obviously no longer had to worry about being judged by her looks, so she'd dyed her black hair. She confessed to Anca she had never explored what she wanted to look like before: she'd always worried about looking professional and making it as a scientist. As a black woman, she'd had a lot of hurdles thrown at her. As a vampire, those hurdles were gone. On the down side, she wouldn't be able to go into sunlight without bursting into flame for at least a century.

Anca said, "We've been caring for these creatures for thousands of years. If we do something, even minute, that changes their environment; we want to *know* it won't hurt them. Which is also why you might have to take some dragon fire to keep an elf safe every once in a while."

"Not looking forward to that."

"It is unpleasant," agreed Anca.

"Do you want to go to the sick bay?" asked Derya.

"No, let's finish our work here first. We should feed the dragons. I don't want to be set on fire again because we didn't feed them quickly enough."

Anca put her black hair back in an elastic. The edges were a bit singed. She made a mental note to schedule a hair appointment to trim off the burnt hair before The Gathering.

She went over to a large wooden cart. Inside there was a potbellied pig trying to push open the door. She lifted the hatch and let it loose. The pig sprinted into the trees. Three dragons the size of Labrador dogs set after it. Some of the dragons were pack animals, so they needed to hunt their food. The rest were content to be fed more easily.

Anca took a bag off the cart. It was difficult to keep a hold of, as it kept shifting in her grip. She let the bag fall. Its side split open. Raw meat spilled out. She upended the bag to fully empty it.

More dragons came forth. After a bit of nipping to establish the pecking order, they set to their meal. There was enough food for all. Some, like the dragon that had tried to play with Derya, hunted their own food within the conservatory. Others, the smallest breeds, the ones that could fit in the palm of your hand, didn't eat meat. Those fed off the berries, insects and other plant life within the conservatory.

Anca watched as a fifty-pound dragon she had nicknamed Monarch came forward. The dragon was colored exactly like a monarch butterfly. She nudged a chunk of goat with her nose before encasing it in flame and then smacked it down with apparent satisfaction. Sometimes the dragons seemed almost human. She set about cleaning her snout so her orange colors gleamed.

A pair of bright yellow eyes peered at Anca behind the shelter of a curtain of needles. She clicked her tongue and held up her arm. The griffin took the invitation. Patterned in grays and browns, the four-legged creature glided through the air silently. Similar in stealth and appearance to their owl cousins, griffins were about the size of house cats.

Landing on her shoulder, he nipped at her ear, his feathered tail tickling her neck as it wrapped around her. On silent wings, he flew back to his perch. Meanwhile, an elf wearing a hat that looked like a mushroom cap scurried for the safety of the pine as well. Looking like tiny people, elves were dirty savage creatures that lived under trees. This one probably had a burrow dug among the roots of the pine.

This conservatory was the only place any of these creatures were safe. Anca tried to remind herself about that when she started feeling guilty about keeping them here. This was the charge of vampires: to protect these creatures from humans. Humans didn't understand that these creatures should be preserved, not eliminated.

Vampires made great care-givers. Getting a face full of flame from a dragon wasn't pleasant, but for a vampire, it also wasn't fatal. Veia, or The Mother, had announced that she'd realized this thousands of years ago during The War of the Last. She had pledged that she, and all her immortal children, would safeguard these "mythical" creatures.

"Okay, we just need to chuck a couple bags of root vegetables and charred meat that way." Anca pointed over a line of tall pines. She turned to Derya. "You know what? You do the first one. I know you must be dying to try out your strength."

Derya took hold of the bag and swung it like a softball pitcher before releasing it. She grunted with the effort. It sailed through the air and just brushed the top bough of a forty-foot pine before it disappeared from sight. "Awesome," she murmured.

Anca took hold of the second bag and casually tossed it through the air. It cleared the pine by ten feet. Anca watched it land thirty feet farther away than Derya's.

Derya looked at her with her mouth open.

"You get stronger as you age." Anca said.

They crept toward the pine and pushed aside the lower branches. In the distance, an ogre was sniffing the closer bag. Great, stupid creatures with a face like a toad, ogres were easily angered, so it was best to feed them at a distance. As long as Anca had worked at the conservatory, she'd never gotten an ogre to be friendly. She could calm them down with food, but she'd never touched one without the intent of subduing it.

"Oh look," Derya said, with her head tilted. An elf was approaching. "Hello."

"I wouldn't --" started Anca.

The elf lashed out at Derya, scraping the length of her forearm.

"Ow! Asshole," Derya said clutching her arm.

Anca shooed away the little creature.

"They're vicious for being so small," said Derya.

"Very territorial. That's why it is best to let them approach you. Preferably while holding food or pebbles." Anca examined the cut. "Let's rinse this out."

They went over to the river. Derya plunged her arm in the icy water. She winced slightly.

"You'll heal," Anca told her.

"Stupid Hollywood," Derya muttered.

Anca could understand her agitation. Most new vampires felt the same nowadays. If they were isolated from their kind, at first they learned from movies that any injury they got as a vampire would heal instantly, but that wasn't the case. Vampires heal more quickly the older they are. Younger vampires heal faster than they did as humans but far from instantaneously. A broken bone would take a couple days to heal for a new vampire. For someone like Anca, a two-thousand-year-old vampire, a broken femur would take less than a day.

"Alright, let's go to the sick bay." Anca deposited their cart in a storage closet near the exit.

When you were in the conservatory you completely forgot you were underground. Between the amazing setup and the magickal illusions, the environment was very convincing. The gurgling river was real and filled with real fish. The pines and cedars were real. Almost everything was real. The ceiling was covered in illusions that made it look like an actual sky. The walls were covered in murals that moved a little, just enough to confuse an inattentive eye.

They did what they could to keep the creatures safe and happy. Qamar had taken to playing his saxophone for the gryphons. (The horse-sized versions of the half mammal half bird creatures.) They loved his music. It looked like a bizarre concert. Who knew gryphons loved jazz?

They were finishing stowing away the cart and marking down what they'd fed and what they'd fed them when Tadashi and a small group of visitors came in through the door.

"Hey," said Anca.

Tad gave a small bow as way of greeting. He was in charge of taking care of the dragons in their Japanese conservatory. Those dragons ate elephants, not pigs.

"Hello Anca, Derya," said Ayiana, Tad's wife. Her strong face shone with approval.

Anytime Ayiana was in France, she stopped by the conservatory. She had quickly grown to like Derya. New vampires were rare. It was even more rare that one would choose to work, their wealth being such that they never had to. Rarer still was a vampire that wanted to work in a conservatory. They had the greatest need but the fewest volunteers. The sexier jobs of security, intelligence and field operatives always got the most recruits. But no one had many. The halving of their population a few centuries ago had left them shorthanded on almost everything, struggling to survive. Plus, becoming a vampire was a potentially lethal process for both parties. About forty percent of the time, the human died in transition. About ten percent of the time, the vampire died trying to turn the human. A human had to be something special for a vampire to risk his life for. More often the human would just be asked to be a consultant and paid handsomely.

A unicorn wondered toward the group. Anca went back to the storage closet and handed apples and lettuce to the new guests. She offered a piece of lettuce to the stallion. He approached slowly. He knew Anca -- she'd been feeding him since he was a foal. The herd, or glory, of unicorns held back. Unicorns were naturally wary, part of why there was still a small glory in the wild that had as yet gone unnoticed. The other reason was Anca's previous job, field work.

Field work had always been a risky job. It ended up being more about bloodshed than preservation. After two thousand years of violence, Anca had decided the only time she wanted to see blood was at lunch, breakfast or dinner... maybe a snack.

It was just as well. Field work had become very technical in the last century. Satellites hadn't been a huge concern at first: they just learned their paths and made sure they were under cover when they came around. But soon, hundreds of satellites had become thousands and that was harder to avoid. And they didn't just take pictures. Satellites could sense density and heat... keeping the creatures outdoors had become impossible. Thankfully they now had bigger conservatories and more of them. The one Anca was in had three chambers, each about the size of an NFL football stadium.

The rest of the glory of unicorns slowly came out of hiding. A foal approached Derya and her apple. It sniffed it suspiciously then took it from her suddenly. She giggled.

"Tad, you think you can show these people around without anyone getting eaten? We need to go to the sick bay." She pointed at her face and Derya's arm.

"Of course." His voice was deep.

Anca and Derya went through the underground tunnel that connected the conservatory to the main building. The sick bay was in the lower level of the main building. Isobel was waiting for them. She was one of the rare trueborn vampires. Anca remembered when her birth was announced. It was a short five centuries after Anca had been turned. Her father had been an Ancient and her mother was almost as old as Anca. Isobell had struggled with her identity growing up. She'd never had the chance to be human. It was a world she didn't know.

Human fragility fascinated her. She found focus in studying medicine. Now she ran the sickbay.

"Anca, what happened?"

"Pebbles tried to play fire tag with Derya."

"She pushed me out of the way before I could get tagged as it." Derya's face was covered in guilt.

Isobel held Anca's face in her hands. "You'll heal fine, but we can have you rest on your birthing dirt just to be sure, speed things up. I know you have a lot to do before The Gathering." She turned to Derya and took a closer look at her arm. "Same for you. We should rinse it out first, make sure no dirt heals into your skin."

Isobel's thick, golden curls threatened to escape from their bonds as she carefully cleaned Anca's and Derya's wounds. She insisted on smearing Anca's face with an ointment and carefully wrapping it. She did the same for Derya's arm. "We need to keep the dirt out." Anca rolled her eyes.

"Careful," Isobel said as Derya lowered herself into the healing pod. Isobel refused to call them coffins. "We aren't actually dead," she'd say.

"I think she can manage lowering herself. Her arm was cut, not amputated," said Anca.

Isobel scrunched her round face at Anca, making her look even more like a sassy doll for little girls. Anca scrunched her face back, then wished she hadn't. Her skin was still a bit tight.

"You next." Isobel gestured at the healing pod next to Derya's. Anca lowered herself onto the dirt, feeling it mold around her. "I'll wake you when I think it's been long enough."

A couple hours later, Anca heard a knock on the lid of her pod. Isobel's sweet face appeared when she opened the lid. "You're all set. Derya's going to stay a bit longer."

Anca had no doubt she'd be back tomorrow, insisting she was fine and asking to go back to work. "Thanks Isobel." Anca unwrapped her face and touched her skin. It was back to normal. She decided she'd ask Derya for a report on what she should have done differently with a summary on elf behavior later.

Anca headed to the training area. She could see sunlight through the tinted windows. It was early morning. Trig would be up. He was in town for The Gathering too, and she hadn't sparred with him in a while. He was massive and knew how to throw a punch. She could use a challenge. Just because she was retired from field work didn't mean she had to turn into a sissy.

"Anca!" She was lifted in a crushing hug the moment she stepped onto the mat.

"Trig for Gods' sake put me down." She caught her breath when she was released. "Good to see you too."

"Good to see you. Where's Derya?"

"She cut her arm --"

Trig immediately tensed.

"She's fine. She's with Isobel getting healed up," said Anca.

"Good," Trig exhaled. A piece of dirty blond hair fell into his face when he looked down at her. He tucked it behind his shoulder. "Hey, I heard from Meryem a couple weeks ago. She's doing fine."

"Thanks. I appreciate you telling me." Meryem was an old friend of hers. They'd done field work together but had become a bit estranged since Anca had retired.

"Did you hear there's going to be jousting again this year?" Excitement was written over every inch of his five-foot ten muscular frame.

"They have jousting every year," said Anca.

"Yes, but *this* year, all of The Ancients are coming to The Gathering, and some of them are going to joust." He bit his lip and raised his eyebrows, waiting for her to share in his excitement.

Held in one of the five main castles around the world, The Gathering was a bicentennial gathering (hence the name) of as many vampires as wanted to come. Each castle was located somewhere fairly secure, but with all the extra guests security was a real concern. The Ancients were first-generation vampires, the oldest and most ancient (hence the name) of all vampires. They didn't always attend The Gathering; having all of them attend was going to be quite the occasion.

"You're going to compete?" asked Anca.

"Of course," said Trig.

"Wait, why are they all attending?" asked Anca.

He scratched his beard. "Don't know. It has been a bit of a headache, but I'm confident they've got it covered." Trig used to be head of security. Most of the security they had now been trained by him. He was very proud of his students. He'd left teaching to pursue business and boatmaking, an old Viking passion of his. "Apparently some big news is going to be shared."

"Huh, wonder what that is. Would you care to spar?"

As an answer, Trig swiped her legs from under her. "That's a 'yes' then?" she asked from the floor. Anca and Trig were more like siblings than sire and sired. Many vampires saw them as a couple, which was ridiculous. They had tried dating in the late 1600's, but they just found it weird. Their uncomfortable experiment hadn't lasted long.

Trig feigned a kick to Anca's ribs and then made to jab her in the nose. Anca noticed the kick was a feign just too late and took a big Norse fist right to the face. Her nose made a definite crunching sound. Maybe she was getting rusty.

She grabbed his arm with one hand and shoved the heel of her other hand into his elbow, dislocating it, blocking a left hook from Trig as she did so. She jabbed her knee into his stomach and swung her elbow into the back of his neck. He dropped.

Anca touched her nose. "Ow. You've improved." Her voice was muffled slightly from the blood pouring down the back of her throat.

Trig rose slowly. "I've been training in some new styles. I could show you."

"No thanks. I'm just doing this to stay in shape."

"Have it your way. I think you'd enjoy a couple years back in the field." He looked at the clock. "I should clean up for the council meeting." He held his arm charily.

"Right, have fun with politics," Anca said as Trig turned to leave. "Can you make sure this is straight, first?"

Trig held her face in his hands and then yanked on her nose so hard it nearly broke a second time. It was turning into a rough day for her face.

"Asshole!" Anca shouted swatting him away.

"It's straight." He laughed with a shrug.

Anca touched her long nose gingerly. It did seem straight. "Thanks. Your arm?"

He held out his arm with a look of chagrin.

"Breathe in," Anca told him.

He took a deep breath.

"Breathe out."

He exhaled, and Anca snapped the elbow back in place. He gave a slight groan and moved his arm around.

"Thanks," he said. They touched knuckles in farewell. Anca headed off to the showers. By the time she was dressed, her nose was completely healed.

She felt like some food. The feeding areas were near the sick bay, so she swung in to give Derya her assignment first. Derya gave an understanding nod and accepted her extra work.

The feeding area was divided in two. Live feeding and "to go" options. Vampires preferred to drink blood right from the source, but it was far more practical to bottle it and store it for later. They had gotten creative over the years, too. Nate, the chef, had come up with some blends. He even took requests. Anca had asked for a smoothie that mixed her two favorites: blood of a vegetarian and plums. Nate had been happy to comply. Others began making requests, much to Nate's delight. He now had a small seasonal menu.

Her Romanian heritage really shone in her flat. Large, colorful flowers covered tapestries and pillows. A giant painting of the mountains of her homeland backdropped an iron khopesh (a nod to her Egyptian heritage) that graced her fireplace mantel. Everything made you feel comfy and energetic at the same time.

She kicked off her Aztec-patterned canvas sneakers and swapped her distressed black skinny jeans for sweats. She picked up her crumpled copy of *The Broken Wings* by Kahlil Gibran.

She wasn't usually prone to love stories, but Kahlil's writing was more poetry than story. Add that to the beauty that is the Arabic language, and Anca couldn't resist. She nestled into her overstuffed couch and buried her toes in the small mound pillows. She was nearly done with the short volume when there was a knock on her door.

A bright smile spread across midnight skin popped into the door. "Mind if I come in?"

"Not at all." Anca scooted over on the couch to make room.

Tall and gorgeous, Ode's lithe figure glided over to the couch. She picked up one of Anca's throw pillows embroidered with a three-petaled purple flower and tucked it under her arm. Ode was in charge of hospitality for the upcoming gathering. She was there to make sure the guests stayed blissfully unaware of how much was going into keeping them safe and entertained as they gorged themselves on anything they could ever want. She had just come from the council meeting Trig had run off to hours ago.

"Are you just getting done?" asked Anca.

"Yeah, what happened to your hair?"

"Pebbles tried to play with Derya."

Ode slumped onto the couch. "Is she okay?"

"She's fine. I pushed her out of the way before she could be tagged "it." How was the meeting?"

"It was pretty heavy." Ode slumped deeper into the small pile of pillows she was forming, her voice low with fatigue.

"That bad huh?"

"You don't know the half of it," said Ode.

The door opened again. This time it was Anca's best friend, Lita, that came in. "Heard you walk by. How was the meeting?" Lita settled into Anca's outstretched arms, perfectly at ease on Anca's lap.

"Terrible, by the sounds of it," said Anca.

Lita looked at Anca's hair. "What happened to you?"

"Pebbles tried to play with Derya."

"We need to schedule you a haircut," she turned to Ode. "What happened?"

" Veia was asked to step down," said Ode.

"What!" said Anca and Lita together.

"By whom?" asked Lita.

"Why?" asked Anca.

"Marcial. He said he'd been asked to," said Ode.

"Who asked him to?" asked Anca completely confused.

"You know… he never actually said," said Ode, as if realizing it for the first time.

"I can't discuss this sober." Lita hopped up and darted out the door. Her suite was one floor down.

"There was also some talk about the library, but it kind of got buried by Marcial's thing," said Ode.

"Understandable," said Anca. "What's going on with the library?"

"Security is way outdated, as usual. It was completely down for fifteen minutes the other week. Etena almost had a fit. She and Goran will be making a formal request at the next council meeting for an updated system."

"Fifteen minutes? That's really concerning. Someone could have broken in in that time," breathed Anca.

"That's what Veia said. She told them to make a formal request and at the next meeting they'll be going over it and give them the appropriate funds. You know, supposedly," said Ode.

Lita walked into the room holding six bottles of wine.

"All of our secrets are in that library we need to keep them safe," said Anca.

"That's what Etena said," said Ode taking a bottle from Lita. "The library's security was down for fifteen minutes," Ode explained to Lita.

"Well that's not concerning," said Lita sarcastically. "Tell us more about this ridiculous request of Marcial's."

"Apparently him and "others" think it is time for a new ruling structure. Just want to ditch what's been working for nearly ten thousand years," Ode took a swig from her bottle. "I thought Nuru was going to tear his head off."

Lita looked at Anca pointedly. "Nuru was there?"

"Shut it." Anca pointed her bottle at Lita. "Shut it or I'll shut it for you."

"What?" asked Ode. "Oh, right you two used to…" She wiggled her eyebrows.

"Yup," said Lita. "Nuru was offered the position of coven leader in Africa just after Anca took her job here in France. They've barely talked since."

When Anca decided she was going to leave fieldwork behind, Nuru had been supportive, at first. He had expected her to bounce back. It became clear he thought she just needed a short vacation, that she'd return to field work quickly. That hadn't happened. Nuru seemed restless. He didn't like not helping in a more hands on way. When he was offered the position in Africa he had accepted, telling her that when she was ready to get back in the field to come visit him. A huge fight ensued. Anca was insulted that he thought this new part of her life was just a phase. That had been nearly a hundred years ago.

"Drama." Ode sung into her bottle.

"Anca's still in love with him," said Lita.

"Shut up." Anca slapped her with a pillow.

"Physical outburst! It must be true," said Ode.

"You too." Anca threw a pillow at Ode. "Besides what is *worthy* of discussion is the council meeting. What exactly did Marcial want changed?"

Ode put down the pillow. "He just said, and I quote 'I have been chosen to bring an uncomfortable proposition forth to the council. I have been asked, to in turn ask you Mother, to step down.' Which is ridiculous."

"That *is* ridiculous," said Anca. "Where does he... What gives him the right? He's barely a century. He's like an infant trying to tell his grandma she's making the cookies wrong. Fuck you baby, these cookies are fucking delicious without your stupid input."

"That was specific and oddly point on," said Ode.

"Why would anyone think Veia should step down? We owe everything to her," said Anca seriously.

"According to him, she's incapable of change. Basically 'they' think The Ancients can't keep up with the new times," said Ode.

"Bullshit," said Anca.

"I mean... I can kind of see his point," said Lita.

Anca glared daggers at her.

"Hear me out before you stab me. The Ancients are nearly ten thousand years old. Most of mankind's progress they've witnessed was gradual. Changes are daily now." Lita shrugged as she swigged.

Anca narrowed her eyes. "I hate that there was nothing untrue in that."

"That was pretty much the point that was brought up. They're going to vote on it next meeting," said Ode.

"Wait, vote on what?" said Anca.

"On whether or not we should change our ruling structure. A group of council members, including two Ancients, were selected to draft up a few options. They're going to present it after The Gathering," said Ode. "Lahari insisted that we wait until after The Gathering to even contemplate it. The next council meeting won't be for three months."

"Lahari's always been very wise for her age." Anca was surprised by the woman when she first turned in the 1930's. She spoke with a wisdom beyond her years, quickly earning her respect. One of the most educated women in India at the time, the vampire that had turned her had seen that she could be a great asset. He hadn't survived the turning.

"Yeah, it's kind of hot," said Lita.

"She is straight, you helpless flirt," said Anca.

Ode laughed into her nearly empty bottle.

"Doesn't mean I can't look," said Lita.

"You are hopeless," said Anca.

"*I'm* hopeless? You're the one with a fine piece of dick wondering around these grounds, and you're here talking politics. We should come up with a plan." Lita looked at Ode who nodded in serious agreement.

Anca did not like the look they were giving her. "Plan?" Anca was trying not to think of the accurateness of Lita's 'fine piece of dick' comment.

"To get you back with Nuru," stated Ode. She turned to Lita. "We should go to the salon in the morning. Brainstorm…"

"Yes, we can go to Cagnes-sur-Mer. Ria could come along," said Lita.

"She might let us use that new car she's been drooling over," said Ode.

"Ooh, we could do some shopping. I am going to help you pick out the perfect pair of shoes. Your legs deserve a cherry on top, so to speak," said Lita to Ode.

"I could really use a fuck me dress. I haven't had a man in too long. I plan on being on the prowl at The Gathering," said Ode. She looked at the carved oak mantel clock. "I should get going. Thanks." She raised the bottle. "I'll see you in the morning. We'll talk shoes and dudes." She said over her shoulder, walking out the door.

"Ah! A fuck me dress." Lita smacked Anca's arm. "That's what you need! What outfit did he take off the fastest? Wasn't it that patterned kalasiris you wore to The Gathering before last?"

"Did I tell you that?"

"Our rooms were next to each other," Lita stated matter of factly.

"Oh."

"He sounded like he liked it."

"Please stop talking."

"What? I'm sure you heard Olivia. She had a *great* time."

"*Please* stop talking," laughed Anca.

CHAPTER 2

The next morning, after coffee and a quick smoothie from her kitchen, Anca knocked on Lita's door. "This was your idea! If you don't want to go --"

The door snapped open. "Don't be ridiculous."

Ode joined them on their way to the garage. They could see Ria was talking to another vampire through the massive garage door. Anca was always surprised when men *didn't* drool in front of Ria, which wasn't often. She was every car lover's wet dream. She had thick black hair from her Italian ancestry and a petite frame from her Chinese ancestry. Her eyes were deep and dark framed by thick lashes. She had a round face and thin lips. She had curves in all the right places and she loved cars. There wasn't a model made that she didn't know about. She could strip down a model T or a 2018 Jaguar blindfolded.

She and Victor were staring at a 2017 BMW i8. Anca thought Ria might cry. Victor was holding the waxing rag loose in his hand.

"Hey ladies," said Victor. "What can we do for you today?" His biceps flexed as he rubbed his hands together.

"We were hoping to kidnap Ria here for a shopping trip," said Lita. "And maybe borrow a ride?"

"Well, not this one." Ria gave the car a small pat then immediately inspected it for fingerprints.

"Your choice, then." Anca laughed at Ria's reaction. She scowled.

Ria chose a 2017 Porsche 911 that was a blast around the curvy country roads. Ria insisted on driving.

Ode gave mock objection, hooking her thumbs on her suspenders, shrugging in doubt.

"Ode, baby, you aren't getting behind the wheel of this thing. We'll have more fun if I drive." No one could argue with that so, they were staring at the giant Sosno sculpture in confusion twenty minutes sooner than they had planned, even with Ria taking forever to find a parking spot. "I'm not putting my baby just anywhere."

"Goodness, how'd you keep your figure after pushing this thing out?" asked Lita.

Ria had just scowled.

"I don't get it," said Anca. She cocked her head to one side, looking at the sculpture.

"Not sure we're meant to get it," Ode said as she squinted.

"I can't tell if he's in pain or not," said Ria. "Why is he in a cube?"

"No idea." Lita glanced at Anca's hair. "Come on, I can't look at that disaster much longer."

The place Lita brought them to was classy. The stylists were professional and highly skilled. Anca left no longer smelling of dragon's breath.

They swung by some boutiques that Lita's stylists told them they just *had* to visit. They were able to find Anca a dress the showed off what little boob she had and made her gray eyes shine. The slit of the dress was so high, you could see her underwear.

"Seeing as this is officially your fuck me dress, I don't think that's a problem," said Lita.

After looking around, they found a navy-blue blouse with a V-neck so deep it almost went to Anca's belly button to help Anca get Nuru's attention before The Gathering. Lita bought more than anyone, as usual. How her closet was going to fit more shoes, no one knew.

Anca didn't get a chance to try and catch Nuru's eye with her new top. He found her as she was walking across the grounds the next morning. Her shirt had coffee stains, and she hadn't done anything with her hair. She'd just had a short meeting about the diet of some of the younger creatures and how they were due to change over the next couple months. She was reading the files when he grabbed her shoulder.

She grabbed the hand and jerked it forward as she thrust her hips back putting a foot slightly to the side of her. Nuru tripped over the foot causing him to launch over her shoulder and hit the ground with a grunt.

"Nuru?"

"Hey Anca." He smiled easily, as if he always said hello from the ground. He brushed himself off as he stood. He was an inch shy of six foot. He had a close cropped, well-shaped beard. His style was casual business man. His gray dress pants complemented his dark skin. The long sleeve t-shirt was rolled up to the elbows showing off his forearms in a way that was somehow extremely sexy. Anca felt the loafers would look too much on someone else but on him they worked.

"Reports?" he asked, looking at the files in her arm.

"Yeah." She held up one of the files she was still holding. "How long have you been here?"

"Day before the council meeting, but I got in late."

"Oh," *Damn it, Anca, get your shit together. Say something flirty.*

"We should catch up. Drinks tonight at the Old Modern downstairs?" Nuru asked.

"Yeah."

Nuru waved as he walked away.

Wait, what did I agree to?

Normally Anca would have gone to Lita for advice on what to do next, but she was working at the firm all day to make sure the people that would be taking care of her case during The Gathering knew what they were doing. Ode and Ria were leaving for The Gathering at that moment. They'd be pregaming on the jet; they wouldn't be of a mind to give Anca advice. She doubted they'd see her call anyway.

She took a deep breath. Catching up over drinks. This could be a date. She thought it unlikely, though. If he had wanted it to be a date, he would have said, wouldn't he? She decided to wear something that brought attention to her tits but could be seen as a casual night out look. The blouse she had just bought seemed perfect. They'd bought it so she could get his attention. Well, she already had it. She'd figure out if it was a date when she got to the bar.

Her heels clicked on the black marble echoing faintly off the walls as she walked down the stairs that led to the bar. Adagion, from the Russian ballet *Spartacus*, was being played on a grand piano. It created a feel of relaxed sophistication in the grand room. Petra, once a Russian ballet pianist, was sitting at the piano in the middle of the room. His face was filled with passion, eyes closed, fingers fluttering along the keys, his blond hair gleaming. The bar had a completely clear top about a foot thick with lights beneath it so the whole bar looked like a block of light; the standing tables were smaller versions of the same. The bar stools were gold with black leather cushions. The chandeliers looked like modern sculptures of glowing golden hoops.

Anca sat at the bar and ordered two fingers of brandy with a splash of water. Suddenly Lita was sitting next to her. "You needed a drink too, huh?" Lita was holding a wine glass that was almost empty. She wore a white lace off-the-shoulder cocktail dress. Her dark red hair was straightened so that it just brushed her collar bones. Amethysts winked the light into Anca's eyes from her earlobes. Her lips were beginning to stain from all the wine.

"Idiots, the lot of them." Lita was too caught up in her frustration to notice Anca's outfit. "They were going to let that useless woman pass on her child support because she claimed bankruptcy. Nondischargeable debt, you fucks." Lita ordered another glass by wiggling her empty one at the bartender.

A low Norse voice echoed off the walls. "Your substitutes not up to snuff?" Trig had just walked up to the bar. He was accompanied by Sarah and Victor.

Sarah had taken advantage of being a vampire by leaving the reservation she had grown up on and now made her living as a freelance travel writer. Her love of travel was part of why she and Trig got along so well. She was wearing her usual leather jacket and relaxed-fit jeans.

"They are now. Only took all day. If they lose this case I'm going to bite every single one of them. Why are *you* here?" Lita asked him.

"I was just talking to Sarah and Victor about what Marcial brought to the council meeting. We decided we should get a drink." He waved to the bartender.

"Marcial? This is a good place for that topic." Nuru walked in. He hadn't changed from earlier.

Merde.

"That's what we thought," said Victor.

Gods damn it. Anca thought this was quickly getting out of hand. She was supposed to be flirting with Nuru to see why he had asked her to join him for a drink; instead they had a small party on their hands.

"Sarah, you look fierce as ever." Lita winked at her. Sarah smiled. Anca stopped herself from rolling her eyes.

"Hey now." Trig wrapped a muscled arm around his girl. He gestured with his beer. "Nuru, I meant to tell you good job at the council meeting. The extra security measures from the witches seemed really good."

"It's been difficult. Magick is meant to manipulate the mind. Cameras don't have minds, but I think we finally worked out how to trick them. With any luck we'll even be able to keep the animals concealed. They could go outside again." He addressed Anca with his last sentence.

"That would be great!" Her mind immediately buzzed with possibilities and concerns. They'd need more hands to watch the creatures outside. They'd need to be absolutely certain the magick was hiding them. They'd need to make sure their presence wouldn't disrupt the local ecosystems and draw attention... the list was endless.

She was so fixed on her endless stream of new possibilities she nearly lost track of the conversation. Nuru and Trig were talking security. "...Those roof tiles baffle me. You'll have to tell me more about them," said Nuru.

"Not much to tell. They're just reflective and block heat. It will decrease the castle's visibility in thermal scans and confuse drones," said Trig.

"That sounds like you just really simplified a very complex thing," said Lita.

"Basically," said Sarah. "There's a lot of engineering behind it. It was Kennet's idea wasn't it?"

"The architectural engineer, right?" asked Victor.

"Yeah, when he's not busy wooing women, he has some pretty good ideas," said Trig. They all chuckled at that.

Nuru was now thoroughly engrossed in his conversation with Trig about their various security measures for The Gathering. The pianist had switched to a piece that sounded like it was from the Georgian era. Anca held in a sigh. *Well this has turned to shit.* She downed her brandy and ordered a double black spiced whiskey. Whiskey always reminded her of her times in the American West. The first sip took her back to that town in Montana. She smiled slightly.

"What are you smiling about?" asked Trig.

"I was just remembering Montana," she confessed.

"When it was still being settled?" he asked.

"Yeah."

"You remember Mathew? You branded his ass. He couldn't sit for a week," Trig chuckled.

"You branded a cowboy?" laughed Sarah.

"I'd nearly forgotten." Anca laughed heartily. "Actually, no I didn't, the look on his face frequently gives me joy. Uh, he was an asshole. He kept branding other people's cows with his own brand and then claiming they'd stolen them. No one could disprove it, and he was such a thug, no one dared face him directly." She sipped her drink remembering. "Nuru didn't you fight a guy in Madrid with a brand once?"

"I did. He was very upset about his face." His laugh was deep, you could almost feel it in your own ribs.

Just like that they were exchanging old stories. With so many memories, it was easy to get stuck in the past. The drinks flowed, the laughter got louder and the smiles wider.

After too many hours, they started to calm down. Lita dismissed herself and stumbled away. Trig excused himself and wrapped an arm around Sarah, helping both of the ladies up the stairs. Victor had taken over the piano and was playing some Alma piece.

"I suppose I should be off," said Anca.

"Well it was good to see you," said Nuru.

"This was a good idea." She started to leave.

"Anca?"

"Yes?"

"You look great."

"Thank you. You too." She turned before he could see her blushing.

Back in her flat, she let her thick quilt envelop her. She didn't even bother to undress before falling asleep, mulling over the night's events. She regretted it in the morning. Not because she had a hangover (another vampire bonus was that she avoided them) but because of her face. She looked like a drugged-out whore. Her makeup was smeared, and she had indents where the body chain had cut into her ribs all night.

"Ugh," she said looking at her reflection.

Anca stepped out of her shower and changed into jeans and a black tank top. She found Lita in her sitting room with a cappuccino and a black coffee. She was wearing a loose low-cut cream tank top over a light gray bralette, stone washed boyfriend jeans and Jimmy Choos. "I just had a horrible realization this morning." She said.

"What was that?" said Anca taking the black coffee.

"Were you and Nuru trying to be on a date?" her face was covered in concern.

"Honestly… I have no idea." Anca sipped her coffee.

"Oh shit. I'm so sorry." She sat back in her chair. "I should've known. You were wearing the blouse…"

"Don't worry about it." The coffee was warming her up, and her damp hair was starting to drip down her neck. "He said I looked great when I left."

"Guys are so confusing." Lita pushed her air-dried waves out of her face to sip her cappuccino.

"I know."

They sat a moment, enjoying their coffee. "Sorry," said Lita again.

"I'm probably just getting my hopes up. It's been years."

"Why the sudden interest? You guys broke up and haven't spoken in almost a century. What changed?"

"Seeing Derya latch onto this life with everything she has… There's a hopefulness to her like she thinks anything is possible. For some reason, when I thought of that, I thought of Nuru and how optimistic he can be. Even with being optimistic, he doesn't lose sight of reality." Anca shrugged. "I wanted Derya to have that kind of perspective. I want me to have that perspective. Then I realized I missed having him around."

Lita nodded. "Derya made you realize that it wasn't just the mind set but the person you missed."

Anca nodded.

Lita contemplated her cappuccino, deep in thought.

"How did he ask you?" Lita looked over her cup. "For drinks I mean."

"He asked if I wanted to catch up."

"Ooh, that sounds like friendzoning," said Lita apologetically. "Yet he said you look great… You'll just have to wear the dress at The Gathering and see if anything happens." She shrugged and sipped her drink.

"Yeah, I suppose." Anca drank her coffee. "You know what we need to do?"

Lita looked at her.

"Pack," said Anca.

"Packing day it is. I need another one of these. You'll help me pack first." Lita got up and walked out without seeing if Anca was following. Of course, they would do Lita's packing first, as it would definitely take the longest. Anca smiled and followed.

Where Anca's floors were a polished walnut, Lita's floors were covered in a thick white carpet. Anca took off her socks, and Lita kicked her heels toward her overflowing shoe closet. Anca saw that she hadn't unpacked the bags from their shopping trip. Lita grabbed Anca's cup and walked into her kitchenet.

"I found out there was another topic of discussion at the council meeting," said Lita.

"Oh?"

"Werewolves are disappearing in the Americas." Lita said over her shoulder. "They asked for assistance in retrieving them or at least finding out who took them."

"Did they get it?" asked Anca.

"Etena brought up the Vampire Werewolf Alliance of 1684. Part of it states we *have* to help each other in these kinds of situations. There was some heated debate, but they got the help."

Vampires and Werewolves had made peace centuries ago. The witch hunts of the seventeenth century weren't just for witches. Vampires, werewolves, anything supernatural was targeted. It was part of what sparked taking the protection of magickal creatures more seriously. Working together, some vampires and werewolves fell in love. Etena had been one of them. The werewolf she had fallen for hadn't survived to see the alliance signed: something he had fought hard to make happen.

Lita handed Anca her coffee and sat down at Lita's distressed white table.

"I guess that would be a bristly point for Etena. What was his name again?" asked Anca.

"Fulton. A Scottish beauty."

Anca gave her a look.

"Just 'cause I wouldn't fuck him doesn't mean I didn't appreciate what he had going on."

"Fair enough." Anca laughed. "I wonder what they'll find."

"Either drunks or a conspiracy," said Lita. "Apparently some thought it was connected to The Ancients that went on holiday last month."

"We don't know they went on holiday," Anca said.

"They were due for a vacation --"

"Yes, but they always told someone where they were going. They just vanished this time."

"They haven't been gone long enough to worry. We'll find where they went when they get back won't we?" said Lita.

"I guess we will," Anca countered.

Lita narrowed her eyes at Anca who narrowed her eyes right back.

They spent the morning packing and drinking coffee. At lunch time they went to the feeding room for a fresh lunch. Anca was directed to an elderly man around seventy years old. She noticed some navy tattoos on his arm and asked him about them. He told her about how he was a fourth-generation naval officer. He told her about how his son and grandson were both in the Navy and carrying on the legacy. She was told about a mission in Russia and how he'd stopped a bayonet from taking his friend's life. The resulting infection had lost him his left arm. She didn't want to point out the missing limb. Often amputees didn't like to talk about how they lost a limb. Sometimes they found it refreshing for someone to ask about it directly. Al was fine talking about his injury. He had been put in a home a few years ago: he hated it. When the vampire came looking for volunteer feeders, he had signed up right away.

Being a feeder was a good life. They got paid well, but that was only part of the appeal. Getting bit didn't get you high per se, but it did relieve you of all your pain while the vampire was feeding on you. For someone like Al, elderly, in pain and lonely, being a feeder was a great option. Several times a day, he got visited by people like Anca who were happy to see him. Vampires would listen to the stories his own children had long grown tired of hearing. It also meant for a couple hours of his day, he didn't feel his arthritis, he didn't get phantom limb pain, he didn't have headaches. He got to eat as much as he wanted of the best food you could think of. Al liked thick steaks, well-aged cheese, and bourbon. Not things that you typically find in retirement homes.

Anca began to feed after several minutes and encouraged him to keep talking. She was happy to learn about him. She liked developing a relationship with the feeders. She didn't want them to feel like food.

After she'd been feeding a moment, he went silent. He wasn't hurt; he was just enjoying the experience. She didn't feed for long. She didn't like to take too much from one person. Al might be visited three more times today. They had caretakers to make sure the feeders never got too low on blood. Feeders were also only allowed to work four days a week and no more than three days in a row. It was a pretty sound system. There had been instances of feeders dying, usually ones that had come from the street or ones that had been fed on by rogue vampires that didn't know how to control themselves. The punishment for killing a feeder was pretty severe, so those instances were rare.

Lita was waiting outside growing impatient. "You were talking to them again, weren't you?"

"Always. You don't need to be so short with your feeders," said Anca.

"I'm not being short; I'm being… efficient," said Lita. They started down the hall. "You don't need to find out the life story of every feeder you suck on."

"And you don't need to treat every feeder like a blood bag," said Anca.

"I do not!" said Lita truly offended. "I respect them. They're the reason we get to eat. I just don't see why I would need to coddle each one every time I'm hungry."

"Respect for your food gives you a better respect for life," said Anca.

"That is so Nuru's philosophy poking through. Sometimes I forget how good he was for you. You were kind of depressed before you guys got together. It's nothing on you. After the witch trials we were all frazzled."

Anca had started to protest.

"Plus, with your history, no one can blame you. You went through hell as a human."

"And you didn't?" said Anca.

Lita slowed her pace.

"We all learn to move on." She muttered. They walked out onto the grounds. Trimmed hedges and a meticulous lawn stretched out around them. A fountain bubbled somewhere to their right.

The grounds were completely walled in. They were far in the country but the vampires preferred to keep a low profile. Even the feeders were carefully selected. They were housed in the main building. Anca and Lita descended the grand stone staircase out the back toward their building, one of two smaller buildings on the grounds.

"We are such cheery vampires," Anca said with a small grin.

"We will be tomorrow. We leave on the same chopper, but you're riding in with Etena the next day. I get to take a limo with a few choice guests," Lita added a little bounce to her stride as they walked across the grass.

"Which makes you a very happy blood sucker I'm sure," said Anca. Anca had to change and make some last-minute checks before she left. She wanted to make sure everyone knew their jobs, specifically the environmental controllers.

"What I'm *not* happy about are the new safety protocols. We need to give blood to cross the barrier the witches put up. All the technological stuff I'm fine with. Go ahead and scan my ear, eye, palm, whatever. Don't make me bleed so I can get in the front door. Who do they think is going to try and attack us anyway? The boogey man? The Blood Brothers? I repeat myself." Lita waved her hand with a chuckle.

"No, they're dead, but there are plenty of others that could try and get in. Some vampires think humans are beginning to rediscover magick. Extra magickal barriers makes sense," said Anca. She held the door of their building open.

"Doesn't mean I have to be happy about it," grumbled Lita.

"We could all use the peace of mind. Technology is making our discovery inevitable. France already uses ear scans to keep tabs of its citizens. One of these days, they are going to notice that a hundred of their citizens don't age. When that day comes, we will be targeted," said Anca.

"And it will be the seventeenth century all over again," said Lita quietly.

Anca faced Lita; they were outside Lita's suite. "Until that happens we are going to keep our creatures and ourselves safe and thriving. Okay?" said Anca.

"Okay." Lita gave Anca a tight hug. "I'll see you tomorrow."

Anca gathered her files from her home office before heading to the conservatory.

The environmental changes were Anca's biggest concern, so she pushed through a door with ENVIRONMENT stamped on it in white letters. She wound her way through a few cubicles then knocked on Mitchel's door. "Hey Mitchel --"

He just about jumped out of his chair.

"Sorry, are you okay?"

"You just startled me. I don't know if I'll ever get used to how fast you guys are," he said, checking he hadn't spilled his water. Like most people that worked this sector, he was human. The vampire population was fairly low. They couldn't do everything. They offered humans well-paying jobs, scholarships, legal pull for family trouble, whatever they needed in exchange for discreet help.

"I just wanted to run over a few things for the next month. You got a minute?"

"Yeah, yeah." He half stood gesturing to a chair for her to sit down in.

"Thanks. I know this is your first time being in charge of a conservatory on your own for this long, and I like to be thorough. I really care about those creatures." She opened her folder when she sat handing Mitchel some papers. "These were the numbers we had discussed before. Has anything changed? Any of the meters moving somewhere we didn't think they would?"

"No, no, everything's fine. We got this. Those meters are right where they should be. You can enjoy being away for a while. We humans can keep the meters where they need to be." His voice was quiet and rushed.

Anca questioned him for a few more minutes and then popped her head into a couple more offices, basically asking different versions of the same questions. She checked with the electricians, the vets, the nutritionists, the landscapers, and the feeders. She ended up running from office to office for four hours. She felt the need to wind down before heading back to bed. She went into the conservatory itself.

Her feet knew this place by heart. Without thinking, she moseyed her way past the fairies staring at their reflections in a pond. One was fashioning a lily into a skirt. Anca found her way to the gryphons. The gryphon she had watched earlier was perched on a branch studying her quizzically.

Anca took a small piece of jerky from her pocket. The gryphon flew down, silently landing on her shoulder. Four sets of claws gently dug into her skin. She handed the jerky to him, and he ate greedily. She scratched his chest.

She knew she'd only be gone a month, but she already felt herself beginning to miss the conservatory. This was one of the few places in her life that offered her peace and purpose. That's something hard to let go of. She produced a small ball from her other pocket. The gryphon perked up, ready to pounce. She threw the ball high in the air. With a great swoop of his wings, the gryphon flew into the air after the ball. Anca could have stayed for hours, but she could feel her long day catching up with her. After a final pat on the head for the gryphon, Anca went back to her suite where she was soon asleep under her quilts.

CHAPTER 3

Anca wasn't considered a high-ranking guest, so she didn't get the bullet proof glass clad vehicles like The Ancients or some of the sect leaders did. But she did get the helicopter, at least for part of the trip. She and Lita were leaving with a couple other vampires. Anca was exhausted from her time at the conservatory when she climbed in the helicopter. She'd only slept two hours. None of them bothered putting on the headsets. Vampire hearing meant they could hear each other without them and that the headsets didn't do much good muffling the sounds of the helicopter.

"They better not drop my luggage!" Lita shouted.

"I'll be happy if we just don't crash!" Anca had had to strategically jump from a hot air balloon once. She did *not* want to relive that experience.

The view of the south of France was spectacular. There was so much green. With how much the world was changed by man in the last centuries, it was reassuring to Anca to see there were still places in the world that were at least a little like they used to be. The mountains were taller in some places, shorter in others. The rivers weren't as blue anymore. The plains were a little browner. The sky a little grayer. But the people were more connected, and diseases were fewer. Not to mention toilet paper.

Anca was traveling from France to Florence Italy. From Florence they would meet up with more vampires and board a plane to Romania. Once in Romania they had cars to bring them the rest of the way to the castle.

Across from them sat Hanare and Isobel, one of the oddest couples Anca had ever met. Isobel gave Anca a wave. "How is your face feeling?"

"Perfectly fine," Anca said.

"Hun, you must have done something wrong," Hanare said seriously.

Isobel looked at Anca with concern.

"Look at her face! Something is wrong!"

Isobel scanned Anca's face as if trying to find what was wrong.

Anca gave a small shake of her head.

Isobel's expression indicated that she caught on that her husband was joking, and laughter spread across her face. You wouldn't know it to look at her, but she'd once revealed to Anca that she had struggled with her identity for most of her life. "Angsty," her parents called her. She and Hanare had met in Hawaii at a luau. She said it was the first time in all her centuries that she had ever laughed so hard.

At one-point Hanare tried to start a game of charades. Seeing a full grown six-foot Samoan man trying to act out bunny rabbit was hilarious. His wife was in stiches by the time they landed. Hanare threw her over his shoulder the moment they were unbuckled. Her thick wavy hair brushed the back of his knees. She was still laughing when Anca entered the awaiting plane. The vampires on the plane obviously thought Hanare carrying his laughing five-foot two wife was also hilarious. Nearly the whole plane was laughing when Anca boarded.

She knew everyone on this flight. There were the pigment twins Hada and Janelle, so called for their vibrant hair. Hada sported long seafoam green hair. Janelle had an impossibly bright shade of red curls just shy of her shoulders. They would forever look like children and not just because they were turned when they were fifteen. When they had been turned, they had been near death due to anorexia. Only the bond of sisterhood had given them the strength to survive the change. They were both turned toward Isobel openly laughing at her situation. Hanare dropped Isobel and picked up Janelle, much to everyone's amusement. Even Orinda was laughing. She worked as a sort of secretary in Italy. Her head was shaved, and she was wearing her usual turtleneck blazer look. She always looked serious, even when laughing.

Tadashi was talking to Wayne and Nate in the back. Nate gave Anca a nod of recognition. He was merely smiling. He had been turned in his late forties. There was a dusting of gray in his beard. Wayne was laughing openly. His smile could light up a room. He had nearly disappeared under his seat. He was so small Anca thought he could fit. Anca knew him from a yoga class of his she had taken.

One laugh in particular caught Anca's attention. A deep, rich laugh that tickled her ribs and made her heart skip a beat, then beat very fast.

Nuru was on the plane.

She should have known he would be: she had seen her travel plans a few times before now, but somehow, she hadn't paid close attention to the guest list. She had paid attention to the entertainment and the food. That didn't mean her heart didn't clench at seeing a young Italian woman sitting in his lap. There were obvious puncture marks on her outstretched arm. Nuru had blood on his lips.

Nuru looked up at the newcomers. His expression changed.

"He has to eat," Lita whispered in her ear.

Anca nodded and sat in the first open seat. Lita sat across the aisle. Anca looked at her, confused. They always sat next to each other. Lita pointedly busied herself with her carryon.

Nuru was suddenly at her side. "May I sit?" he asked.

"As long as it doesn't disrupt your digestion."

Beyond Nuru, Anca saw Lita freeze and close her eyes, as if praying for patience.

"I forgot to eat this morning. I haven't fed directly in a long time. I figured we were celebrating…" He sat down slowly. "You want any?" He gestured at the woman now being fed on by the pigment twins. They fed on humans delicately because they were afraid of hurting them. They knew what it was like to be malnourished and light headed. They didn't want to inflict that kind of panic on someone else.

"No, I'll just get a bottle of something."

"What would you like?" Nuru began to stand up again.

"Um, I think I'm feeling like drinking with my drink." Anca smiled. He was right, they were celebrating. Her job was done until she got back to France. She could cut loose until then.

"You got it." He went to the front where there was a full bar.

A small pillow hit Anca in the head. "What the hell?"

Lita slid in the seat Nuru had just left. "*What* is wrong with you?" She lowered her voice so Anca could just hear it. "You are trying to get back on that dick. He is obviously up for it."

"Really?" Anca looked at Nuru getting something from the fridge.

"God, you're hopeless." Lita vacated the seat so Nuru could sit.

"Here you go," he said. Anca took a champagne flute. The bubbly spirit had been mixed about fifty-fifty with blood, by the looks of it.

"Sorry if I seemed judgmental," Anca said to the back of the seat in front of her.

"Don't worry about it. We both work too much. Sometimes it's hard to cut loose."

Anca gave him a smile. She definitely got a bigger smile back than the situation called for. "How has Africa been treating you?" she asked.

"Things are all right. We actually seem to be making some headway. It's nice to get out of the city."

Anca knew Nuru spent most of his time pushing papers and working politics in Kampala in Uganda. His job was delicate and stressful. The vampires had been trying to form an alliance with witches across the globe, part of their plan to come out of the coffin gradually, so to speak. In Africa that had proved more of a challenge than other places. Some African witches still performed a type of magick that required sacrifices to their ancestors. The louder the sacrifice screamed, the more likely the ancestors would hear them and the stronger the spell would be. Nuru had been working on persuading them to end this practice before approaching them about an alliance. It was slow going.

"How's the conservatory?" asked Nuru.

"The dragons have calmed down some since Tad showed up. The large gryphyns still favor Qamar. Brenna's going to transfer to the South American conservatory soon. We'll miss her. The elves didn't bite her as much as anyone else." Anca had begun to smile without realizing it.

"And yourself? You forgot how *you're* doing."

I suppose I did. "I'll always love the smaller gryphons, my little fruit dragons. The environment is pretty stable. The guy in charge while I'm gone seems capable, a little nervous but I think he'll do fine."

"I'm glad things are going so well. Now," he raised his glass, "a toast. To The Gathering and a good time." They clinked their glasses and drank. "We are no longer talking about work. We are here to have a good time. We don't get to let go and just be vampires very often."

"Alright, what do you want to talk about?" asked Anca.

"What I want to talk about is fun times and carefree fun, but I've been thinking about the Blood Brothers a lot recently," he said.

"Way to bring the mood down," said Anca.

"I don't know why they keep creeping into my thoughts."

"More like nightmares."

Nuru nodded in agreement.

"They are dead."

"And you're okay with that?"

"They tortured themselves for kicks and broke apart our family. Yes, I'm glad they're dead," said Anca.

"I'm sure it was hard for you to hear about it. We were watching that church at the same time but stopped. Do you know why?"

"Exhaustion. You can only spend so many decades being paranoid before you stop looking over your shoulder. After a while, I stopped *wanting* to look. Sometimes I miss it though."

"What?" Nuru shifted in his seat to look at her more directly.

"Being out. Out in the world not just cooped up in the --"

"Shots all around!" boomed Hanare.

Janelle came bounding down the aisle, her green hair bouncing, and handed Nuru and Anca each a shot. Janelle raised her own shot expectantly. Anca shrugged and the three of them drank. After takeoff, Hanare resumed his attempt at charades. Anca thought he was trying to mime whale. Turned out he was trying to mime penis.

During the short flight, Hanare convinced Wayne to try tequila, and the pigment twins got in on the charades. Every passenger was having a difficult time breathing by the time they landed. Anca hadn't laughed that hard in years. Hanare let Isobel leave the plane on her own two legs. Wayne wasn't so lucky. Wayne was also much wigglier. Hanare dropped him just before he stepped onto the ground. Wayne was fine. He did have trouble standing up. Anca thought his lack of balance had more to do with the nine shots of tequila she had just watched him drink than the fall.

Even vampires could get tipsy after enough drinks. Especially ones still getting used to the heightened tolerance. Many made of the mistake of thinking they couldn't get drunk. Watching them learn that they could was one of life's simple pleasures.

They were all going to stay at Hotel Noapte that night. The vampires owned the hotel, one of their many sources of income. An entire floor could only be accessed by keycards. That floor had a feeding room, and all the rooms were for vampires only. Light tight rooms were specially fitted for with private pathways to the garage so they could avoid the human guests if they chose. This week, all the guests were vampires. As usual, most of the service and lower level jobs were staffed by humans who thought they were just hosting a private event, not vampires. The hotel had been receiving guests from around the world on their way to The Gathering. As Anca and the rest of the flight went into the hotel, numerous vampires were going out to get into cars, limos, or helicopters for their final leg to the castle. Anca gave smiles to all of them and even stopped to hug a few friends. Some vampires made the trip in one stretch, but for the sake of discretion most were asked to come gradually so Romania wouldn't suddenly be swarmed by vampires. They were trying to stay under the radar, after all.

Anca barely had time to shower in her room before there was a knock on the door. With a towel wrapped around her head she opened the door. It was Lita.

"You need to find something sparkly to wear. They're having an impromptu recital in the ballroom."

Lita was already dressed in a shimmering emerald green cocktail dress. Her hair was in perfect vintage waves pinned back by sparkly silver barrettes. Anca hoped Lita wasn't planning on jumping; she'd pop right out of that low sweetheart neckline.

They quickly dried and styled Anca's hair and threw some makeup on her face before squeezing her into a sparkly black flapper dress. They giggled like school girls as they effortlessly sprinted down the hallway. Their heels made soft thudding noises against the plush carpeting. Anca stopped a moment inside the thirty-foot double doors to take in the spectacle.

Six crystal chandeliers, each as tall as a man, hung between spiraling pillars. Crystal glasses on golden trays were being offered by waiters in white dovetail suits. A giant stage dominated the far side of the room. On a smaller stage on the right side of the room a band was playing.

Qamar was playing the saxophone. He was, hands down, the smoothest jazz player Anca had ever heard. His playing for the gryphyns was nothing compared to here where the acoustics were so good. Just like at the conservatory Qamar's music was a flame that ignited the happiness in everyone around him. Petra was on the piano, his usual composer flung aside as he swayed back and forward using his whole body to play the keys.

Anca and Lita watched in awe as a flair bartender made them both martinis. The music changed from jazz to classical. They turned in their seats to look at the stage to watch the ballet that was starting.

Anca saw Willow taking pictures of the ballet. Her dark hair pulled back in a low bun. She looked like a black and white photograph her skin was so pale, and she never wore colors. An artistic choice, Anca supposed. She must have sensed Anca looking. She looked at her and Lita. She pointed at them both and lifted her camera. Anca nudged Lita; they put their heads together and raised their martinis. The camera flashed a few times. Willow looked at her camera a moment, then gave them the thumbs up.

They turned back to the ballet. Irina left the stage when the ballet was done and went straight to Petra, her husband. They had met when Irina was a professional ballerina in Russia where they were both from. He had been the pianist for her company. Irina had been injured when she later joined the army. After she turned, she immediately offered Petra the option of becoming a vampire. He had accepted without hesitation, insisting she was the only muse that could motivate his playing, and without his playing he wouldn't want to live.

Anca tried to focus on the moment. When she looked at everyone, it was easy to get swept away by all the memories they brought up.

"Damn." Nuru had just walked up to the bar. His eyes were glued to Anca, perhaps a bit lower than was proper. He was wearing a black button up shirt with a gray vest and charcoal dress pants. Casually cool.

Anca smiled like an idiot.

"She means thank you," said Lita.

"You're welcome," said Nuru. He bit his lip.

Damn why'd he have to do that?

"Do you want to dance?" asked Nuru.

Lita took her martini before she answered.

"Yes, I would." Anca looked at Lita pointedly. "Hold my drink, won't you?"

"I will until it's gone." Lita took a gulp of her martini.

The music had changed to swing. Qamar was now on the trumpet. The little band he led was playing "Quatier Latin" by Die Golden Sieben. Anca had danced to this very song at a Christmas party in 1934 in Germany. Nuru grabbed her by the waist, then as if remembering, held her right hand. They moved with the music back and forth. Soon Nuru was tossing Anca into the air. His feet were a blur as he got caught up in the music.

Nuru loved to dance, especially swing. Anca twisted with the beat, following Nuru's lead she kicked her feet high. For a moment she thought she might kick Willow in the head. She was dancing with Nate much more wildly than Anca was dancing with Nuru. Nate looked completely lost. Ask him to make a consommé turducken or Béarnaise sauce, no problem. Ask Nate to two step, you might want to wear a helmet.

The crowd was loving the swing dancing so the band played a few more songs before switching genres. After a waltz and a foxtrot, the stage lit up for the next performance. This time an opera singer took the stage. Her voice was positively ethereal.

Anca and Nuru had gone to a standing table where Lita was chatting to Trig, Sarah close to his side. His hair was pulled back and he was wearing a button up shirt with dress pants.

"What's got you so dressed up?" Anca asked. Trig rarely dressed up outside of work.

"I thought we might as well," said Sarah, wrapping an arm around Trig. She had ditched her usual casual attire for a red satin dress. It was simple but flattering. She didn't dress up much either. Anca didn't always understand them as a couple. They had much in common, but they spent most of their time apart. Anca thought it was strange how two people could be in love and be apart from each other so much, but for them it worked.

"Your bodies work great together," said Lita to Anca and Nuru.

Nuru laughed at that.

Anca smiled at the floor.

"I'm going to make a request," said Nuru leaving the table. He walked over to the band.

Lita now gave Anca her full attention. "So?" she asked expectantly.

"It was nice. We do dance well together," Anca confessed.

"I like him," said Trig. "Always have. He treats you well."

"Why'd you guys break up, again?" asked Lita.

"He kept prying, wanting to know everything about me," said Anca.

"Oh no. A man that wants to get to know you. The horror," said Lita.

"I've been thinking lately. I could stand to open up more. Maybe I should take some time off…"

"Yes!" said Lita and Trig together.

Sarah laughed at their unexpected agreement.

"It would be nice to go back to Africa for a bit. I haven't been there in years. Morocco has changed so much," said Anca.

Nuru came back to the table. "You'll love it. The bridge between worlds. We could go after The Gathering. Maybe you'll let me show you the remains of my old master's home in Benin."

"That sounds great," said Anca with a smile.

"We all need to remember our past," said Lita. "It helped shape who we are. Helped," she pointed her finger at them, "not dictated."

"Here, here," said Nuru.

Anca thought about how different their backgrounds were. Anca had been born in the shadow of the Romanian mountains. Trig had been a Viking ship maker. Lita had been a midwife who was exiled after she was discovered as a vampire, among other reasons. Sarah had been a struggling student on her reservation. Nuru had been a sort of apprentice for a philosopher. Perhaps explained why he tended to be more serious than most of the people in whatever room he was in.

Most of their backgrounds were tragic. Trig had lost his sisters. Lita had the love of her life die in her arms. Nuru was torn from his family in a war. Sarah had grown up without drinkable water for miles (not the end of the world but still a depressing fact of life). Anca had lost her family to a conflict between her clan and a neighboring one. Incredible. Though you'd think those scars wouldn't hurt anymore, her heart would still twinge when she heard a hammer strike bone.

Our past can shape us if we let it, but our choices are our own. We are each a spirit that we shape with our actions. Each day, each choice is a chance to redefine ourselves. Every cell in our body is reshaped in months. In a single year, you can completely change yourself, physically, emotionally, mentally, spiritually. As Anca had lived a hundred lives, she'd changed herself countless times. Her attachment to her past was purposeful.

"To loving the past enough to move on," toasted Trig.

"Cheers," said Anca. They all raised their glasses.

A Persian man with a perfectly trimmed beard and thick hair approached the table. "Nuru, we need you upstairs."

"No, we are celebrating. No work until after The Gathering," he said.

"I'm afraid I must insist. I need you to come too Trygve," the man said.

"Why me?" said Trig.

"Can you please just come."

"Is something wrong?" asked Lita.

"No."

Anca thought his easy smiled looked a bit forced.

Nuru turned to Anca. "Sorry."

"It's okay," said Anca.

Trig kissed Sarah's knuckles. "Don't have too much fun without me," he said.

They watched the men leave. "I wonder what's actually going on," said Lita in a rare moment of complete seriousness.

"I don't know," said Anca. Her head spun with possible answers.

CHAPTER 4

A gold tassel swayed from the ornate menu Anca was scrutinizing. She was sitting in a large room with pillars. A waiter poured spring water into her water goblet. "Are you ready to order miss?"

"Yes." Anca ordered a simple breakfast, fruit and oatmeal. A minute later another waiter brought her coffee. He made the coffee in a French press at her table. His movements were elegant; she remembered him, as he'd been working at the hotel for years. He presented her with the cup and left the press on the table.

She was reading *Il Machiavellismo Per Tutti* by Giovanni Galleggianti, a philosophy book in Italian. She sipped her coffee and listened to a twenty-person handbell choir playing near the self-serve coffee. Lita plopped into the chair opposite Anca.

"Good morning," said Anca, continuing to sip her coffee, not looking up from her book.

"Morning," said Lita. She snatched the menu and began looking at her options. "I'm starving."

"Busy first night?" asked Anca.

"Maybe." Lita wiggled her eyebrows at her menu. When the waiter came with Anca's food, Lita ordered a mimosa and blood cheese omelet.

"Really? That can't wait four hours?" asked Anca.

"What? Like Nuru said we're celebrating. Did you hear from him after he left yesterday?" She sipped her drink.

"No." Anca took a bite of her food. "I fink he might haf already left."

"For The Gathering?"

Anca nodded, still chewing.

"I'm convinced he would have taken you to his room last night if he hadn't been pulled away. I guess you will need your fuck me dress after all."

Anca stared at Lita with narrowed eyes, swallowing her food angrily.

"Hey, that's why we bought it. All you need to do is let him see you in it," said Lita.

"I hope you're right," said Anca.

"Of course, I'm right."

Anca looked at the clock. "I leave soon. I'll see you tomorrow."

"Okay. See you," said Lita.

Later Anca checked out of the hotel. The heels of her Aztec print ankle booties clacked, and her silver thigh chain bounced against her thigh as she made her away through the lavish lobby. As grand as this place was, she knew a bigger and more beautiful home awaited her.

A butler opened the door to the sleek black car that waited for her outside the double glass doors. Inside sat Etena with a thick volume her lap. Her traditional tattoos peeked out from her button up shirt. Anca got a weak wave in response to her hello. She looked at the cover of the book Etena was engrossed in. *Interview with a Vampire*. Anca had to smile. She put in her headphones as they pulled onto the road and blared her latest find in the Indie Pop genre.

After over an hour in their own worlds, Etena put her book down. She waved at Anca who pulled out her earbuds.

"Sorry, I was at a really good part. I didn't want to put it down." Etena apologized.

"We've all been there. Don't worry about it. I heard you'll be presenting at the next council meeting?"

"Finally." Etena grumbled, her head back. "We've been asking for updated security for years. We desperately need to scan and electronically file all the books... Somehow the money always goes... somewhere else." She waved a hand. An effortlessly elegant movement from her years of hula when she was a human girl.

"I get that." Anca had her own frustrated dealings with the financial department. "There always seems to be money for the frivolous shit and never for the important things."

"They just have a different idea of what's important. That failure really has me spooked. Fifteen minutes blind. Most of The Ancients acted like they couldn't care less. At least Mother cared. Who knows though." Etena exhaled. "We could put the best, most reasonable proposition forward, and they could still vote it down. Maybe we're presenting to placate ourselves. Goran was already making lists. He could do this presentation by himself," she smiled.

"What?" Anca tilted her head.

"What?"

"Do you like Goran?" Anca inhaled. "You do!"

"No, I do think he likes me though. Work has gotten a bit awkward. He keeps helping me with stuff."

"Is something wrong with him?"

"No…"

"Than what is it?" pressed Anca.

"I just don't want work to be weird," Etena said exasperated.

"Sounds like it has already gotten weird. One date can't hurt much. The Gathering's as good a time as any. If it makes you feel better, we could bump into him at a group thing. Lita and I can feel him out and tell you what we think?"

Etena nodded. "Maybe that would be best."

"No offense, but neither of you get out much. Maybe you just don't know what to do around each other because you don't know what to do around anyone."

"You may have a point." Etena confessed, gazing toward the mountains.

They both looked at the scenery properly for the first time. They had driven out of Transylvania and into Walachia. Most people thought of mountains as cold, hard, harsh. The mountains of Romania were welcoming and not just because Anca called them home. Green hugged the landscape, blanketing the mountains in a soft quilt of life. Streaks of gray stone peaked through the tears of that quilt just to remind you of the elevation.

The road they were on curved among the scots pine. They took a wide left turn and the trees on the right began to thin and then drop away. Anca, seated on the right, pressed her face against the window. There in the distance was Castle Acasă.

To look at it, you would think the mountains had grown around the castle so perfectly did they wrap it. The castle was made of dark brown stone. There were seven towers; the tallest was no less than twelve stories tall. The roof tiles were a rich purple. Anca noticed they shone more than they had on her last visit.

It had been agreed in 1021 that a grand home should be built for the next Gathering. That this home would be large enough to house a legion of vampires, grand enough that any guest would want for nothing, and hidden enough that they could drop any façade of humanity the moment they stepped through the door.

Construction on the castle began the following year. Forty years and two dozen deaths later, the castle was completed. Updates had been made over the years. The front gate was no longer as ornate as it once was but was more secure than ever. It was still beautiful to any eye that looked upon it, but the swirls weren't as delicate. A large stone wall now encircled the entire property. Something that took longer than the castle to complete. And of course, security cameras watched the entirety of the outside grounds. Having cameras on the inside had been considered too intrusive to the guests.

Another twenty minutes of windy roads led them through the front gate. The driver showed his ID and guards quickly scanned the car with mirrors and trained dogs. Anca and Etena had to let the guard scan various body parts and prick their fingers a few times. He poked the needle into a symbol on the guard booth and on the ground before they were let through. The driveway was a vast circle of perfectly raked pea gravel. Anca recalled when it had been a straight dirt driveway. As soon as gravel was invented, the driveway had been changed, by then they also had carriages. The driveway had been changed to a circular shape so that guest's carriages could more quickly get out of the way for the next guest's carriage.

Butlers waited for them at the base of the grand staircase that led to the front door to take their luggage and escort them to their rooms. Anca and Etena climbed the stairs with smiles on their faces. There was nowhere quite like home. They shared a hug before departing to different wings.

Great care had been put into making everything in this part of the castle look old. The highest light fixtures were outfitted with electric candles for efficiency and convenience but any lights within easy view were the real thing. Some vampires, especially The Ancients, still had a hard time adjusting to technology. The Gathering was a time to go back to simpler times, easier times, slower times. The event would last one month. Well, officially. Unofficially this castle would host this party for nearly a year. Many of the guests had already arrived and been partying for weeks.

The second official day of The Gathering was always somber. It quickly picked up to the biggest extravaganza any of them ever witnessed. When you had fifty years and nearly inexhaustible funds to plan a party, it's going to be astonishing.

But a party so wonderful doesn't just happen. Even as Anca was walked to her room she noticed various vampires flitting about trying to get everything done. Every vampire was required to help with The Gathering at least once. You could forgo working your first Gathering, but you had to help with the second. Without requiring the assistance Anca knew this event would never happen. Who wants to spend their eternity working?

If a vampire had a job, it was because he loved doing it. Many vampires, Anca included, worked for another reason: purpose. It's easy to go adrift with eternity at your fingertips. Life seemed to become meaningless. Many vampires came from harsh backgrounds, especially the older ones like Anca. Depression was an inevitable part of eternity at some point. With so many memories of blood splatter and screaming, it was hard to be present in the happy times of life. Anca had found purpose with the conservatory. She was still able to use her skills of being a soldier, but she didn't have to worry much about one of the creatures triggering memories from battle. She liked it that way. A quiet life.

Such serious thoughts were no longer necessary. She had a couple days until that somber second day of The Gathering and she planned on pampering herself. Anca used a large iron key to open the door to her room after dismissing the butler, insisting she didn't need anything more from him. Her wing was considered the Elder Wing. Technology was kept to a minimum. The other wing, where Etena was, had key cards. Here Anca didn't have to worry about the buzz of technology. She had enough of that on a day to day basis. This did mean however, that the bathrooms were old-fashioned as well. They flushed, thank the gods, but you had to pull a chain attached to a lifted tank to do so. The vanity consisted of a pitcher of water and a small sink, no faucet. No shower either Anca would have to call for hot water when she wanted a bath. She loved it.

The thick wooden door was studded with nails. She swung it open. The "room" was more of a suite. A sprawling sitting area was what first greeted her. The floors were tiled with black marble. The walls were made of thick bricks of gray granite. The plush couches were black velvet. Red roses in white and blue porcelain vases were on every table and counter. A fire was burning in a ten-foot-tall fireplace on the left wall. Large Romanian tapestries hung on either side of it. Unlike her flat in France, this suite had no kitchen. When Anca wanted food, she simply had to pull on one of the labeled cords near the door. Guests of the elder wing were told these cords rang bells in the servant's areas, but Anca knew they had been switched to electric years ago. Now, when one of the cords was pulled, a light blinked on dozens of monitors around the castle. Whoever was closest would tap the screen, claiming the task, and then fulfill whatever the request had been.

Anca pulled the cord labeled for food. A maid showed up precisely three minutes later. "How may I be of service?" She held three menus in her arms.

Anca ordered lunch. A sparkling rose water mixed with blood. When the food arrived ten minutes later, Anca had most of her belongings strewn about the room. She thanked the maid and began unpacking, taking special care to properly hang her fuck me dress.

Most of the furnishings were antiques meticulously maintained over the centuries. She opened the large standing wardrobe. Inside were carved wooden hangers topped with stuffed velvet. She grinned; it really was the details that counted.

She sipped her drink while she hung up her clothes, letting herself take her time settling in. Soon enough, she would be caught up in the festivities. She didn't see herself spending much time in this room. She looked back at the wardrobe. A certain dress happened to be hanging right in the middle. Well, maybe she would.

Later that day when Anca felt she had sufficiently pampered herself with a steaming rose water bath, facial, and foot massage, she headed out of her room to the library. The library had been a part of the castle from the first blueprint. It had been one of the main forms of entertainment back then. Now they had a full-sized theatre, a spa, even a few indoor courts for various sports. The library hadn't changed. Taking up the entirety of the Southwest tower, the largest tower of the castle in width, the library was eight stories high. The library from *Beauty and the Beast* came close in size but Anca preferred this library. So did Etena. Anca spotted her next to a growing stack of books halfway up on one of the wheeled ladders on the second floor. It was easy to picture a looming beast next to her. Nothing could get Etena's attention quicker than a well-stocked library.

Technically, Etena was on the fourth floor. The first two floors were kept in almost complete darkness beneath Anca's feet. Those floors housed the most prized volumes, scrolls older than Anca, books larger than a child, and some velum papers that were so frail they were forever pressed between vacuumed sealed sheets of glass so they wouldn't disintegrate. Many were copies, ancient copies. The originals were in the main library where Etena worked.

Anca climbed the spiral staircase that wrapped the center pillar of books. There were five such pillars in total. Everything here was circular. The bookshelves were all curved to allow access to all the books via the wheeled ladders and the all the curves meant the echoing was diffused. The tapestries that hung from the rafters helped with keeping the noise down.

Anca quietly waited at the bottom of the ladder. It took several moments before Etena noticed her. "You just can't stay away from these things, can you?" asked Anca.

"There's a reason I volunteered to work at the library. Maybe in a decade or so I'll have to volunteer to work here. Learn preservation. Work somewhere smaller." She had changed into a short red romper. The swirling tattoos on her thighs on full display.

"I suppose this does seem small to you." Anca looked around. If each level had a floor the square footage would be 1962.5 feet. Not exactly small. "How many books are in the library you work at?"

"I honestly don't think I can count that high. Or have the time to even being immortal." They looked at her stack of books.

"Are you just going to stay in your room the whole time?" asked Anca.

"No," said Etena. "Well… not the whole time. Goran's arriving in a couple hours."

"We talked about this. You shouldn't avoid him."

"I know. I just don't know how to act around him anymore."

"Well we'll have a meeting later in my room if you want. Bring whoever you want."

"Sure."

"Before I get too sidetracked. Do you have any suggestions?" asked Anca.

"Book?" Etena hopped off the ladder.

"Yes."

"What are you looking for?" She put her hands on her hips.

"I don't know… Maybe a retelling, something modern?" Anca tilted her head in thought.

Etena pondered a moment. "You know, I have just the thing."

They moved to the other side of the library and went up another floor where to the newer books were stored. "Dee dee dee dee." Etena scanned the books. "Here you go." She pulled a volume off the shelf and handed it to Anca. "Cinderella. Instead of losing her shoe she loses her foot."

Anca gave her a look.

"She's a cyborg."

Anca raised her brows.

"There are also people on the moon."

"OK, officially intrigued," Anca said with a soft chuckle.

A woman wearing a sleek black dress with a silver chain that had crescent moons at each end wrapped around her waist approached. "Oh, that's a good one. The name was a bit deceiving though. Of the series that is. I thought it would be more about the moon itself."

Anca bowed her head. "Camena."

"Anca. Etena."

Etena bowed her head to the woman.

"Are you here for The Gathering, or did you gain another sister?" asked Etena.

Camena was a moon priestess, a leader of the Nadirians the moon-based religion shared by vampires and werewolves. The religion was based on consistency during times of change. Like how the moon was always there even if you can't see it. For vampires, the religion portrayed their lingering existence as the world changed around them. For werewolves, the religion centered on them focusing on their humanity, even when they shifted. Since werewolves had begun taking up the religion, it also focused more on unifying their two species, existing in peace.

Camena looked every bit a moon priestess. Her hair and skin were snow white. Her eyes the lightest blue. Anca thought of her as a snowflake personified. Oddly Camena hated the cold. This was apparent in the fact that her dress was made of velvet with a high neck and slit bishop sleeves.

"I am here for The Gathering." Her voice was a bit high and always quiet. "Although I would like to take counsel with one of The Ancients at some point."

"Is something wrong?" asked Anca.

"More of us have been seeing blood in meditation and feeling flashes of pain. We fear we are seeing a growing threat. I wish to discuss such things with The Ancients."

"I'm sure Veia would lend you her ear for a time," said Anca.

"I certainly hope so. I approached you, Etena, for a similar request as Anca's. Can you recommend something for our newest sister? She would like to begin learning our history."

"Of course. Follow me please." They headed down the spiraling staircase toward the older volumes.

Anca thought a moment about all the history the lower levels held. She thought about the records that were kept. Somewhere down there was the official record of Derya's turning. Anca realized she hadn't read it yet.

Anca followed them down the stairs to the darkened room.

To a human, the room would have looked as if it was kept in total darkness. To the eyes of a vampire, the room seemed dim with a faint red tinge to everything. The light was less damaging to the books.

Every precaution was taken to keep these records pristine.

Vampires that chose the path of magick for their eternity could become illuminators, record keepers. It was lowly job but essential. Four such illuminators were at work when Anca stepped into the room. One was taking records from a new vampire. The eyes of both were whited over. The witch was touching his fingertips to the other's temple hovering their other hand over an open book. A purple glow emitted from their hand and solidified as words on the page. Anca took a look. This vampire had been turned ten years ago by an Ancient, Briton to be precise. He had been turned in the jungles of southern Venezuela.

Anca turned her attention away. Perhaps it was Camena's comment about seeing pain in meditation or her chat with Nuru on the plane, but suddenly Anca wanted to read some of their older texts. The most ancient texts were on velum thin as a breath sandwiched between UF-3 plexiglass displayed in an upright zig zag. Anca walked slowly, skimming through the texts until she found what she was looking for.

And so the Time of Unity passed and the Mother 9There was a hole in the text.) The Brother for his misguided lust of pain banishing him and his followers from

What? Banished?

Anca read the line again. She knew these people. They were the stuff of nightmares. Had Mother once been connected to them? How far back did their history go?

Anca suppressed a shudder. She moved farther down and kept reading.

In the days of burning the Blood surged in anger. Many perished. The changelings of the moon were used to quench the threat.

Again, not hard to figure out. The witch trials were a terrible time. Vampires had been threatened with extinction, and their alliance with the werewolves was the only reason they survived. Anca crouched down to peer at the text closer.

In the days of burning the Blood surged in anger.

Why was "blood" capitalized? She looked back at the previous text to read further along.

The Blood forever separated from the Mother.

Was there a connection? Where both texts referring to the same thing? Anca shook her head. She was supposed to be having fun, not looking at ancient texts that gave her a headache. It was probably a mistake.

She made for a display of books against the far wall, the newest records of turned vampires. She scanned the page and found Derya's name.

Derya sired of Qamar reborn of the soil of France counseled by Anca.

Anca smiled at the page. Here was her legacy. Her whole life was spread across these pages. If she went back she would find the record of her turning Trygve.

Trygve sired of Anca reborn of the soil of Norway counseled by Veia.

Anca spread her hands against the plexiglass staring at the book below set against the dip of the display to keep the book open. Derya would do well in this life. She was a human with good intentions and now a vampire with an eternity to answer any question she may have. Anca would do what she could to keep her safe, to enable her to keep learning. If only more of the world was interested in learning instead of ruling or standing out. What a better place it could be.

As Anca was walking out she saw a witch putting her thoughts to page. She looked at the page.

In her wisdom, she forbade the speaking of the Blood to the counsel until such ancient threats could be verified.

What the fuck? Anca wanted to tap the shoulder of the witch to question her about what she was recording but never got the chance. The purple glow of the witch's hand went out. She slammed the book shut. "You aren't supposed to be reading this," the witch snapped at her.

"Then maybe you shouldn't be doing it out in the open."

The witch scowled at her and took the thick volume with her to one of the private recording rooms where secret records were supposed to be kept. *She must be new.* Anca followed her with her eyes. "Blood" capitalized again. What did it mean? Why was it being kept secret?

What else don't I know?

CHAPTER 5

Anca wondered the castle looking for friends to invite to Etena's girls' night. Harp music drifted up to her from the wine cellars. Acting on a hunch, she followed the melody to an impromptu concert put on by Kennett the engineer who had designed the new roof tiles. Anca could tell he was concentrating because he seemed oblivious to the fact that most of his face was covered by his dreadlocks. He was a fairly muscular Chinese man with half his head shaved and heavily tattooed. As usual he had a small gaggle of females around him. Anca wondered when the last time he had gone to bed alone was.

There were a dozen five-foot-tall candelabras in the space. The flickering candlelight glinted off Kennet's gages. Anca made her way to a shadowy corner.

"Hello, Anca."

"Hello, Meryem. You look different as always." Both looked forward.

Meryem smiled slightly.

"You still never turn off," said Anca.

"Not all of us were built to retire, Anca."

"The shorter cut suites you, brings out your seriousness."

Meryem let out a short chuckle. A waiter came by and offered them a wine list. Meryem pushed back her blunt bob with a smile and politely waved him away. "You blew my cover Anca. I was trying to go unnoticed."

"Well, I noticed you, old friend. I'm actually here to collect some friends to help Etena with some boy trouble."

"Aren't you dealing with your own?"

"Of course, you would know about that already." Anca shifted against the wall.

Meryem smiled. "I like to know you're safe. I keep tabs on you."

"And I you," confessed Anca. "How was New York?"

Meryem looked at Anca. "How on earth did you find out I was in New York?"

"I have my ways." She looked at Meryem.

"One of these days, I'll be better than you." Meryem turned her gaze to the harp.

They watched Kennet play. From the look on the faces of the surrounding women, he wouldn't be going to bed alone tonight.

"You surpassed my skill years ago, I'm sure," said Anca.

"I suppose it is possible. You are retired. You could have gotten rusty." A competitive gleam was in her eye.

"Come with me to Etena's thing and we'll spar after so you can find out," said Anca.

Meryem thought for a breath. "Fine, lead on."

They didn't stay at Anca's suite long. Everyone had quickly agreed Etena should go out with Goran and see how things went. Meryem and Anca's impending spar took everyone's attention soon after. They had all migrated from the suite to the training rooms. Anca was wrapping her hands her hair now in a long braid. She wore a sports bra and leggings. Meryem was similarly dressed, with her dark hair loose.

"Go Anca!" shouted Lita.

"We haven't even started yet." Anca finished her wrapping and stepped onto the matt. "Any ground rules?" she asked Meryem.

"No permanent damage?" she suggested.

"Sounds fair."

Ode walked onto the matt stopping between them. "Alright ladies." Ode's voice was loud and clear. Anca noticed a group of vampires on the other side of the room stop what they were doing and look over. "I want a good dirty fight. Hair pulling is fine, tit punches are fine. Stop at long-term damage. No eye gouging, no limb ripping, and don't break any major bones either," Ode's voice grew soft and serious. "The day of mourning is soon, and you should look nice for that."

Anca and Meryem smiled at each other. It was true, they shouldn't do anything that would make them look a mess. They nodded at each other and then at Ode.

An audience was beginning to form at the edge of the matt. "No permanent damage and stay on the matt. Agreed?" Ode looked at Meryem, she nodded. "Agreed?" she looked at Anca, she nodded. "OK. FIGHT!" Ode swung an arm down between the two of them before bolting off the matt.

Anca socked at Meryem's nose. Meryem pulled her head back and deflected Anca's jab with her forearm. Anca swiped at Meryem's leg. She jumped up to avoid Anca's attack and to knee her in the chest. Anca turned letting Meryem's knee slide down her raised arms. She twisted so that her block turned into a round house kick. Meryem landed from her jump into a crouch rolling away.

The crowd was growing. Anca had been one of their best warriors when she still worked the field. She was also considered an Elder. It wasn't an official ranking; it just meant she was not quite an Ancient but was now one of the oldest vampires. Meryem fit that profile too, though she was a thousand years younger, only she was still working the field. Her reputation was still fresh. Many new vampires that sparred with her had to be carried to the sick bay where they would stay for days. A fight between the two old friends would, of course, get some attention.

The two women were highly trained and knew each other's moves. Anca and Meryem had trained together for a thousand years. This was both a benefit and a hinderance. Blocking was easier because they could tell what attack was coming. Attacks were harder -- the other was already blocking by the time they landed the blow.

Anca tried to use this against Meryem. She would start one attack and change it halfway through, hoping to through her off. But Meryem was good. She caught on to Anca's new tactic, quickly beginning her own tactic of combining seemingly conflicting attacks and blocks to throw her off. Meryem glanced her shin off Anca's ribs. Anca had turned just in time so that she didn't receive the full force of the kick that would have sent her flying off the matt and losing her the fight.

The crowd was going crazy. Normally, a fight with a well-trained human lasts less than two minutes. A fight with a well-trained vampire can be over in seconds. But Anca and Meryem were too evenly matched. Eventually this would become a battle of endurance. Anca had no intention of letting the fight last long. By the look in Meryem's eyes, neither did she.

"Meryem! Meryem! Meryem!" chanted a group of field operatives.

"Go on Anca!" she heard Trig shout. When had Trig gotten here?

Meryem gave her an opening. Anca knew it was bait, she also knew Meryem knew she knew it was bait. Fighting could get complicated.

She went for it… sort of. Anca landed a blow with the edge of her hand on the side of Meryem's neck, but she put most of her strength behind scraping her foot along Meryem's shin. She blocked the attack to her neck too late and realized it had been a diversion even later.

Anca's foot landed on top of Meryem's, pinning her where she stood. Anca put as much force as she could into a left uppercut. Meryem had been trying to land her own blow. The punch hit her under her chin so hard she would have done a backflip if Anca hadn't still been standing on her foot. Instead they both were lifted off the ground and slammed flat on their backs. Anca flipped up quickly, sprinted to Meryem and placed her foot on her friend's throat.

"Yield?" asked Anca.

"Never," said Meryem, then she smiled. "But you won that one." She raised an arm, Anca helped her up. The crowd cheered louder than ever. Meryem pulled her in for a hug. "I guess you *haven't* gotten too rusty."

CHAPTER 6

The castle was nearly filled to capacity. Just over four thousand vampires were now housed on the grounds. Whenever so many vampires get together, there are certain things that are guaranteed to happen. One of them is gossip. The main topic: Marcial and his request that Veia step down. Alarmingly, no one knew who it was that had put Marcial up to the request.

This realization nearly overtook the topic of who should take over should Veia step down. Some thought it best that they create a new ruling structure from scratch. Others thought they should just modify the existing structure. Many thought the whole thing was absurd. As usual with politics, most talked in circles, offering no real solutions. Anca had chosen to ignore as much of the talk as she could. They would find out the fate of their leadership at the next meeting. There wasn't much reason to fret over it until then. Besides, none of them had a real say in the decision anyway. She hadn't been able to silence her mind, though. *What will happen to them? Who is behind this ridiculous request?* Her mind whirled with questions.

There was a knock on her door. "Let me in!" It was Lita.

Anca pulled herself from her bed, a little achy after the fight. "What do you want?" she asked the door.

"We need to plan!"

She opened the door. "What?"

"We need to plan," said Lita as if it were obvious.

"Plan what?"

"Do you remember our shopping trip? Do you remember what our mission is this month?" asked Lita.

Anca stared at her a minute, blinking slowly.

Lita took pity on her. "You need coffee."

Anca nodded, her eyes half closed. They could have had breakfast delivered to her room, but Anca wanted a view with her lunch, and nowhere had a better view than the dining room in the east tower. They enjoyed their breakfast over a 360° view of the mountains. These mountains were one of the few things that could still make Anca feel small. She'd grown up in the sight of them, not these exactly.

As a girl she'd wake to the smell of wood smoke. Her father would usually be gone on a hunt, avoiding Anca, she knew, despite what he and her mother told her. As the years went by, her brothers had gone with him until it was just Anca and her mother each morning. She'd look at the sun rising over the mountains and feel so small.

Anca stopped herself. That story ended too sadly. It must have shown on her face.

"What's wrong?" asked Lita.

"Just thinking… thinking of growing up here."

Lita understood immediately. "Don't do that," she said firmly. "We're supposed to be having fun."

"I know, Mom."

After ordering a vegetarian and coffee, they got down to business. "I think you should put on the dress today. We know that it will get his attention, but we should talk about how you're going to seal the deal. It shouldn't take much. How are you planning to flirt?" Lita asked. "Guys tend to like something more straightforward, but if you really want a chance at another go you should be a bit coy."

"I don't know… smile?"

"That makes them think you're just happy for attention or give your attention easily. You need to look them up and down. Be interested in what they're talking about."

"I didn't realize girls and guys were so similar in flirting."

"I've had to deflect the attention of many men over the years. I know what not to do to get their attention, so I also know what to do to get their attention."

They agreed that Anca would make her move on Nuru tonight. It was hard to eat between all the giggling. They went to Anca's room to pick up her dress, then went to Lita's room to get ready.

An hour into their preparations, there was a knock on the door. Ria poked her head in the door. "Hey girls, mind if we join?"

"Not at all," said Lita.

Ria was followed by Isobel and Ode. As usual, Ode got ready quicker than anyone else due to her hair being so short. Isobel had so much hair that they had barely begun on hers by the time everyone else was ready. Lita seemed to be concentrating very hard on the task that was styling Isobel's hair. "What are we going for exactly?"

"I want my husband to fall in love all over again."

Lita said, "You two are so sweet you rot my teeth."

Isobel laughed.

"How long have you two been together?" asked Ria.

"Married forty-three years. We have been "together" forty-four years," said Isobel.

"You were only together a year before getting married?" asked Anca.

"I had to have him," said Isobel to her reflection.

"So, what kind of hair style do you think is most likely to make him pop in his pants?" asked Lita.

"Lita!" said Anca.

Ria and Ode were laughing.

"Hey, nothing makes a guy fall in love faster than the mere sight of you making him pop off in his pants," said Lita.

"I thought I was the expert in that," said Ria. They all laughed.

Ode held up three dresses. "Which one?"

"Depends," said Lita. "What are you going for? Are you on the hunt for dick tonight too?"

Ode considered the dresses seriously. "Maybe."

"Then not the middle one," said Ria. "It needs to be clingier if you're going to cover that much skin. You should also consider the day's festivities."

"Which are?" asked Isobel.

"Tightrope walkers, aerialists, singers, musicians, contortionists, fire dancers, and..." Anca tried to remember what else was going on today.

"Gymnasts and escape artists." Finished Lita. "There will also be a walking buffet."

A walking buffet was when numerous feeders walked throughout the crowd. Vampires could feed on them at whim. To make sure no feeder was used too much they switched them out every two hours.

"But that's the entertainment. What will *we* be doing?" asked Ode.

"Watching them," said Lita with a shrug.

"There's also movies playing, jousting, all the courts will be open. You could join the pool party," said Anca.

"Ooh, that sounds fun," said Ode. Ria nodded.

"You know I think I'll watch jousting," said Anca.

"Good, you can join me. Hanare is competing today," said Isobel. Lita had managed to pile her hair in an elegant, yet secure way that played up her dainty features.

"A perfect place for wearing gorgeous dresses," said Lita. "We can see who can distract one of the guys enough to get him knocked off his horse."

"That sounds more fun than the pool," Ria said to Ode.

"Jousting it is," said Ode.

They were the image of elegance by the time they left Lita's room. Just before they had left, a bouquet of gardenias had been delivered. The note said they were from Hanare.

"Rotted teeth," said Lita walking past a beaming Isobel, who inhaled the smell of them deeply before having them sent to her room.

Anca and Isobel were arm in arm as they walked past dark carved wooden sconces. Lita led the pack in her own sweeping gown of pale lavender. She wore a ruby choker and bracelet and red stilettoes. The contrast brought attention to her red hair and bright lips. Her boobs were hoisted impossibly high, giving her unnatural (if minimal) cleavage. Anca almost felt sorry for the jousters.

The jousting was being held outside under connected circus tents. All together the tents covered the space of three American football fields. Each of the support poles were wrapped in cloths of the colors of a different country. Numerous flags and ribbons had been pinned to the fabric to show support by different vampires for their favorites. Anca took a moment to add to the Romanian, Egyptian, and French pillars. Soaring stadium seats flanked the competition area, also decked out in a blinding array of colors. Anca was impressed that the girls earned more than a few stares against such a backdrop.

Isobel broke from their group to find her husband. He was standing next to a giant black gryphon whose back was level with Hanare's shoulders. He was in full warrior garb with obvious nods to his heritage, a collar of red feathers, a belt of embossed disks and the helmet he was holding had a fan of red then purple feathers. Anca watched Hanare make a big sweeping bow to his wife and produce another giant gardenia from seemingly nowhere.

"Call the dentist. I need an appointment." Lita whispered to Anca, making her way past her to grab some seats. Anca smiled and followed.

Isobel joined them a few moments later, beaming. Lita pretended to be annoyed by exhaling loudly. Isobel swatted her in the face with her gardenia.

Anca accepted a small bag of freshly popped popcorn from a man who was walking around with a vending tray. The tray held a small dragon that belched flame at a covered copper bowl that contained the kernels. He kept having the stop the dragon from eating all the popcorn.

"Trig!" Anca waved him over.

Trig bounded over, his armor clanking. "Come to see me win?" said Trig.

"I wouldn't count your wins yet," said Isobel.

"Hanare's got nothing on me, the youngster."

"Don't be too sure," sang Isobel as she swung her flower.

"Just wanted to wish you good luck," said Anca.

"None needed." Trig ran back to his mount, a navy-blue creature that looked part horse part deer with shining silver horns that corkscrewed backwards. Trig pat the creature's neck and checked the saddle. Jesting effortlessly with passerbys and bragging of his impending victory. For a moment Trig remined Anca of her brother. So sure of himself.

No, he was cruel and unyielding. Trig is kind and optimistic. Very different, she scolded herself.

An announcer's voice boomed throughout the arena calling the attention of the crowd reminding the competitors to ready themselves. Lita and Ria were talking strategy in front of Anca. She shook her head. She scanned the crowds looking for Nuru. She was starting to feel ridiculous in her dress, half her ass cheek was hanging out the slit.

The crowd cheered when the announcer proclaimed the official start of the competition. A great murmur went through the crowd when the first competitors were announced. Two Ancients.

Anca knew some Ancients would be competing, but she was still nervous. Ancients were treated like fine china among vampires, frail, irreplaceable, priceless.

Her worries were lost to her cheers in no time. The two Ancients bashed each other with reckless abandon. The crowd drew a collected inhale when one Ancient was run through with a lance then erupted into a cheer that hurt Anca's ears when he withdrew the lance and hit the other Ancient in the head with it. The Ancient that had been run through won the match. They bowed to the crowd and made way for the next competitors.

Trig and a new vampire Anca didn't know yet took the field. Trig won against the woman easily. It wasn't really a fair fight: she was barely over a century; he was over a thousand years old. They, too, bowed to the crowd before making way for the next competitors.

Lita checked her boobs. Ria gave her a nod of approval, and then they turned to watch the next match.

Hanare and Veia took the field. Isobel gave a smile to her husband. It faltered slightly when she saw who he was paired against. There was no way he could win. She recovered quickly, cheering louder than all the rest.

As everyone had suspected, Hanare lost quickly. On the second pass, Veia unseated him sending his feathered helmet flying through the air. He was a gracious loser. He yielded after a short scuffle with swords on the ground. He drew her into a hug that lifted her off her feet before the winner was declared. Veia lifted his arm when they bowed to the crowd. Both were laughing the whole while.

The next competitors took the field. One was adorned in colorful beads and feathers arrayed so that he looked like some angel of war. The other knight left their helmet on and was dressed in simple armor with no adornments riding a dappled unicorn. The battle was intense. Over and over they passed each other, their lances splintering time and again. The knight in black armor lost their shield but kept fighting dodging two more blows before unseating their challenger. They fought with swords on the ground. Although the man had been the one knocked from his horse, he gained the upper hand once on the ground. The black knight fought more energetically but with less precision. The knight was pinned to the ground after being disarmed. It had been a close fight, but the black knight rightly yielded.

The crowd erupted once more. The black knight removed their helmet at last to reveal… Sarah. "That's my girl," Trig roared above the din. Anca laughed and clapped with the crowd.

Trig and Sarah changed out of their armor and joined Anca in the stands. "You both fought valiantly. Was that your first jousting competition?" Anca asked Sarah.

Sarah nodded.

"Now I understand Trig's excitement," said Anca.

Trig kissed Sarah on the top of her head with his arm lazily draped over her shoulders.

"I didn't tell you my good news," said Trig. "At the council meeting I got approval for developing a blood substitute. I was going to tell you at the hotel, but I got pulled away," said Trig.

"Why did you get pulled away?" asked Lita.

"Security: that's why Nuru got pulled too. There were some questions about the border."

Sarah spoke, "It all turned out fine."

"What was wrong?" asked Anca.

"Nothing was wrong," said Trig. "They had a feeling the security should be upped, and they wanted our input. You know how seriously they take security for these things."

Anca thought back to the twelfth century when she had been part of the security for The Gathering. She, other fighters, and witches patrolled the grounds with swords, axes, and bows and arrows. Before satellites and cameras, dragons, gryphons, and tethered ogres were also used for security. They weren't as concerned about being seen as they were about anyone seeing them and living to talk about it. As the years passed and technology became more inescapable, The Ancients had insisted on staying completely out of sight. In Gatherings past, their insistence bordered on paranoia. Only in the last twenty years had they begun to relax at the insistence of newer vampires. They showed them that they could use technology to their advantage, take the offense in a sense, but the need to go unnoticed was still strong.

"Anyway, it all turned out fine. Nuru had the witches add a couple layers of magick of his own design, and I pointed out a few weak spots for my guys to work out," said Trig.

"Speaking of Nuru," Lita leaned over into the conversation, her boobs dangerously close to escaping her dress. "I don't see him anywhere, and we haven't been able to get a single guy knocked off his mount."

Ria was nodding sadly over Lita's shoulder. They agreed they'd check out the pool party, saying that a bikini would do just as much for Anca's cause as a dress, if not more.

She put on her black bikini that had a band of red Aztec print on the bottom of the top and top of the bottom. The small black tassels added a fun element to the suit Anca hadn't been able to resist. It was simple but flattering. With so little to hide behind her athletic build shone. She was especially proud of her butt. She gave it an appreciative glance before collecting the girls and heading to the pool. Lita joined her in a ruffled white eyelet number that draped her shoulder and played up her petite figure. Ode shone in a bright yellow one piece with wide open sides. Ria wore a strappy black monokini that made her bosom look fantastic. Isobel was off with her husband. Who knows what she was or wasn't wearing.

The pool was in one of the lower levels carved out of the rock of the mountain. The original idea had been to bring the tropics to the mountains. Every notch of the exposed rock was filled with sprawling palms or colorful bromeliads. A ledge on the wall had been left bare so the vampires could cliff dive off the forty-foot-tall platform. There was even a swim up bar that was serving drinks with tiny umbrellas. Ria and

Ode bee lined for it. Anca and Lita followed. She swam through the main pool. It had been the only pool at first at six hundred thousand gallons, and then they added the bar and diving well that was fifteen-feet in diameter and thirty feet deep. The pool also had a spiraling sixty-foot waterslide and numerous waterfalls, a few of which had alcoves behind them. Anca saw a couple disappear behind the falling water as she made her way through.

Passing the half-moon jacuzzi, Anca passed between two palms and entered the bar area. The stone was left barer here with only the occasional hibiscus or orchid coloring the gray stone. In the water, fish of varying colors made of light swam among the vampires, and what looked like fireworks burst in the water's depths. It was as if you were swimming through a galaxy made of living rainbow light.

The bar itself was separated from the pool via a three-foot-thick aquarium that wrapped around the bar and the half-moon jacuzzi. Inside were colorful tropical fish and some other aquatic creatures that mankind had forgotten about. An abtu swam lazily along the bottom edge of the enclosure, a deep red fish striped in glowing yellow. Passing it overhead was a salmon-looking fish whose fins glowed purple and were poisonous to the touch. Anca didn't worry about the other fish being hurt, these species had lived side by side for eons.

The pool was nothing but fun. Dozens of vampires jumping, splashing, laughing, and drinking the day away. She swam up to the bar and sat between Ria and Lita. Ode and Ria were openly flirting with some guys drinking in one of the small alcoves in the bar area. After they got their drinks, Ode gave Anca a wink, and they swam over. After a few minutes, it was all hands and laughter.

"What about you?" Anca asked Lita. "You looking for love while we're here?"

Lita took a deep breath. "Hmm... Love? No. Lust? Probably." She wiggled her shoulders.

"How you can give such great relationship advice while jumping from one lover to the next... I have no idea."

"It's a gift." Lita sucked on the bright pink straw of her drink. Suddenly her drink frosted. She looked at it quizzically, then looked over Anca's shoulder with a sultry look. Anca looked to see who was trying to flirt with her.

Long blond hair tied back in an elegant braid dripped water down pale skin. He turned around. A coy smile played on his long face. He made his way to the bar slowly, careful to keep his martini above the water.

"Ladies." He gave them each a long, appreciative look.

"Urian," said Lita.

"Heavens help me." Anca gulped her drink. Urian and Lita were both audacious flirts. After they were done flirting with each other, they'd often play wingman for each other.

"Your freezing skills have improved." Lita raised her glass, showing him his work.

"I have many skills. Secrets waiting to be shared, if given the correct..." he looked her up and down. "Motivation." His last word was a breath.

"Good Lord," Anca muttered. She signaled the bar tender. "Whiskey, lots of it."

"Now Anca, there's no need to provide an excuse for when you slip away with me. Anyone that sees me knows I'm reason enough to be swept away from reason." He gave her a half smile, eyes sparkling.

She looked at him, then at Lita, then at the bar tender. "Like I said, lots of whiskey."

The bar tender nodded, an understanding look on his face.

"If you won't let me stimulate your..." he raised his eyebrows, "I'll stimulate your brain. What are your thoughts on the possibility of restructuring our ruling structure?" He sat on the stool next to Lita, his game over.

"I find it insulting," said Anca.

"I know you must find the request insulting, but you can't say it is unfounded," said Urian.

"Thank you," said Lita. They both turned to look at Anca in full.

"Outnumbered, am I? Let me ask you this. Who asked?"

"Marcial." They said in unison.

"No, Marcial said someone asked him to do this. Who asked him? Why? Why don't we know who made the request? If it *is* so well intentioned why keep that a secret?"

"It is concerning," Urian confessed. "The point holds true however. Times are changing. Here." He reached forward and chilled Anca's glass. "It's still easier if I can touch the thing I'm trying to effect. I've only been practicing three hundred years."

Magick is nothing more than concentrating enough to manipulate the energy around you. The more you practice concentrating, the more you practice magick, the better you get at it. Having thousands of years to practice could make vampires formidable magick wielders. It was part of what made The Ancients so powerful. Some had over five thousand years of practice.

"Well, you do better than me." Anca looked at her frosted tumbler. She'd dabbled with magick off and on in the past few hundred years but couldn't do much more than make something feel cool or warm to the touch. Vampires had to pick magick or fighting. Both took a substantial amount of time and effort to master. Fighting had more substantial results sooner, so many vampires went with that. Magick had a slow learning curve. Like Urian said, it took centuries to be able to do anything physical. Most magick was different kinds of illusions or mind manipulation. That's where the idea that vampires could control the minds of humans came from. It wasn't magick at all, it was psychology.

They're beautiful, intriguing. You want to believe them, so you do. To look at a vampire, you see a human where everything is a little better. They're slightly prettier than if they were a human, and they sound better, they smell better, they move better. For some reason, people are more likely to do what you ask if they are attracted to you.

"What a strange illusion it is to suppose that beauty is goodness."

"What?" said Urian.

"A Leo Tolstoy quote," said Anca with a wave of her hand.

"I like it," said Urian.

"How are your illusions?" asked Lita.

Urian conjured a white snake that wrapped itself around her shoulders.

"Beautiful," she said.

The snake was patterned with flowers instead of regular scales. With a twitch of his wrist, the snake disappeared.

"You are definitely improving," said Lita.

"Many of my skills have improved."

"I take it you'd like a chance to show off those skills." Lita put down her drink and looked around. "Picked out anyone yet?"

"Not anyone I have a chance with." He made eyes at Anca.

"You're right, not a chance," Anca pointedly turned away.

Lita and Urian went off to flirt with anything breathing. *At least the fish are safe.* Anca went to the diving ledge. She saw her maker at the top. She climbed the boulders, passing a small group of vampires belly dancing on one of the ledges. There were four of them dancing, two of which were crouching, playing drums. Three of the dancers were ladies of various height and build, clearly from different backgrounds. The fourth was an elegant young man with dark skin, tight curls, and deep brown eyes. He moved as gracefully as the others, his eyes closed more often than not. He had small orbs of fire circling his wrists and flowers in his hair.

"Veia!" Anca called.

Veia turned around and pulled her into a warm hug. "Anca, so good to see you. Care to join me?" she tilted her head toward the water.

Holding hands, they jumped from the platform. They raced each other to the bottom. Veia touched the blue tiles a half second before Anca. Pressing her feet against the bottom Anca straightened her legs quickly, launching herself through the water. Veia surfaced next to her, smiling, her dark curls flattened from the water.

"Join me. We need to catch up." Veia dove just under the water's surface and mermaid kicked to the edge. Veia walked out of the water. Her skin was much darker than Anca's, and she had curves Anca would never have. With her bubbly personality, the only way you could tell her age was her eyes. They didn't have wrinkles: they were dark and deep. Looking at them, you believed that they'd seen millennia. They'd seen some shit.

Anca joined her next to a small fire pit. Veia pat dried her hair with a towel, her curls bouncing back to level with her chin.

"How are things?" asked Anca.

"Fantastic, everyone's having a great time," said Veia.

Anca tilted her head.

"You mean, how am I doing after the meeting?"

Anca nodded.

"Better than you might expect." She lay down on a lounge chair.

"You weren't shocked?"

"No, I've been expecting something like this for a while now. He was right. Times are changing faster than we are. Faster than I am surely. The only constant is change."

"So, you're considering it? Stepping down?"

"Absolutely, I would have stepped down myself eventually, I'm sure. Like I said, I've been expecting this for a while. I could use a vacation and not just the year off I get here and there." Veia looked toward the dozens of vampires laughing and splashing. "Whatever I can do to ensure this," she waved a hand, "continues. I love my children. I would do anything for them."

"I know," said Anca. She too looked around. Urian and Lita were chatting up some of the belly dancers. She could hear them suggesting something about trying the moves horizontally. Daran was moving away from the group to find his wife clearly uncomfortable.

"I guess I'm pissed that someone could think you... incompetent."

Veia laughed, it was genuine and joyful, like her. "I hope not. I was thinking they found me outdated." She looked at Anca seriously but with a broad smile on her face. "How are you? Are you still enjoying *retirement*?" She made air quotes around the last word.

"What's that," Anca made air quotes, "supposed to mean?"

"You call it retirement, but you still work quite a bit."

"True. But it is good work, I haven't had to kill anyone in a while, and I like that."

"It does get taxing. You know some of the newer vampires are drinking coconut water. It can be substituted for blood. Not permanently. Humans will use it for emergency transfusions. With Trig's work, progress will go more swiftly. Maybe we can, if not eliminate, significantly wean back our consumption of human blood."

"Huh, wouldn't that be something?" Anca had a thought. "Walk with me?"

Intrigued, Veia wrapped herself in a saari and followed Anca out of the pool area. When she was sure they were out of earshot of the pool, which took several minutes, Anca spoke.

"I read something disturbing in the lower levels of the library. Something about a brother being banished and Blood."

Veia stopped in her tracks.

"It also talked about the changelings of the moon being used to banish the threat. I thought it was referring to the witch trials, but judging by your reaction it is more than that isn't it?"

"The werewolves hunted down a threat: that's all anyone needs to know. They saved us from more than humans in those days. I should tell you that much. I couldn't tell you, you know why."

Suddenly Anca knew what the other threat had been. She understood why it had been kept secret. "He was there?" she choked out the question.

"I never heard but -- they weren't kind to them, they killed everyone, even their feeders. Those were the orders." The last sentence came out like a confession.

"How many people were told?"

"Not many, maybe a dozen that weren't directly involved. It was centuries ago. Many have died since.

"The witch trials were going on. We were barely keeping our heads above water. and then we learned we were being attacked by another enemy at the same time. If we had told everyone we were being attacked on two fronts, it would have been panic. It could have finished us. It almost did." Veia's face shone with strength and conviction. She wasn't apologizing; she was explaining to her child a fact of life that they were now old enough to know. Anca had to accept this truth. So, she did.

"I understand. I don't like it, but I understand," said Anca.

"I never liked it either. But it was our best option. If some of them somehow survived..." She raised her eyebrows and shook her head. "Every Ancient will have to be held accountable for the decision, anyone that knew, the werewolves too. It could very well shatter us if not exposed correctly."

Anca nodded. Faith would be lost in The Ancients. The alliance with the werewolves would splinter. If the attack ever became known, it could cripple them.

How many friends would I lose if they ever found out I knew?

"Is that why all The Ancients are here?"

"I don't want to spoil the surprise."

"I won't say anything," Anca promised.

"I thank you for that. No, it's something else." Veia turned and continued walking. "Our population is still depleted. I think we rely too heavily on humans. We suppress their memories and make sure money changes hands but eventually one will remember or decide nothing we give them is enough. It worries me, but we need to eat and we don't have the numbers to do everything ourselves. The humans fill the positions vampires refuse. How many vampires do you know that would willingly be a cleaner?"

"I see your point."

"In one breath I complain that we rely too heavily on humans, and in the next I must confess it is a reliance of our own making."

"A conundrum."

"Quite," Veia quirked a smile.

They passed a large grandfather clock. "I suppose I should get ready. I'm to wear a ridiculous ensemble."

"You have to wear it?"

"People expect certain things of their Mother. As I said, I'd do anything for my children, including wearing something far too poufy." They parted ways with smiles on their faces. Anca had a gnawing thought. *What else don't I know?*

CHAPTER 7

The Welcoming Day. The first day of The Gathering when all guise of humanity was abandoned and pleasure was the only pursuit. The entertainment stunned and the guests caroused. It was Anca's favorite day.

To accentuate their vampirism, the dress of the day consisted of bright red lipstick and outfits that made quite the impact. Anca's dress was milder on the showy side of things but flashy enough that it had passed Lita's inspection. It consisted of a red lace jumpsuit that could have passed as a second skin with layers of sheer black fabric draped down her sides that went in just enough to cover nipple. The black lace garter on her thigh held a stiletto dagger. Her back was completely exposed. Derya's eyes had gone wide when she saw her. "Do I have to wear something like that?" After Anca had assured her she did not they found her a black satin dress that ended just shy of her knees. Lita put both of their outfits to shame. A black lace tube dress with red sheer draped cross ways from one shoulder. Her nipples, or anything else for that matter, were not covered.

"I wonder what The Ancients will do this year," Lita said as they walked down the hall arm in arm with Derya. Anca had insisted on bringing her with. Every year The Ancients had some aspect of their outfits that set them apart from everyone else. They were never told beforehand what it was. but somehow no one else ever had that element in their outfit. Anca suspected mind manipulation.

They were off to one of the many parties that would be going on all day. The Welcoming Day was more informal in that there wasn't a set schedule or any rituals they had to partake in. All the guests were free to meander and enjoy themselves. It was mostly a day of reunion. But with so many vampires and so many different parties going on at once, it was hard to say hello to everyone.

They had decided on starting out their Gathering experience with a bang. Anca wanted to wow Derya. They were going to the dancing flame party. They approached the room, their bare feet silent against the tiled floor. An exotic mix of Indian and Trap music called to them, luring them in.

None of them had bothered with doing their hair and why was apparent the moment you saw the door. In place of a door was a constant sheet of water cascading down. They stepped through it, immediately soaked. The fire wouldn't really hurt them, but it would ruin their clothes and with the amount of fire in the room it was necessary. The floor was covered in sand, another precaution against the fire. So much fire. Anca laughed when Derya's mouth fell open.

No lanterns were lit, and every window was closed, yet the room was filled with living light. Dragons lazed about on the iron railings of the balconies randomly spewing fire as it amused them. Guests were greeted by a woman wearing a three-foot crown set aflame levitating a large hoop of fire with her hips. Next to her was a man with a mohawk of fire and two thick ropes set alight. And they were the least of them. Farther in were men twirling giant cubes of fire and women with fans that sparked with each flick of the wrist.

Anca smiled wide, exposing her double upper fangs.

"That's right! Let loose!" Lita shouted over the heavy base. She smiled so broad her upper and lower fangs were on full display.

Derya gave a hesitant smile; she was still getting used to exposing her fangs. Lita grabbed them both and dragged them onto the dance floor. Before she knew it, Anca had lost herself to the pulse of the room. The music shook her bones, and any thought she'd had burned away with each sway of her body. She was drunk off the vibrations.

Lita began dancing with an Indian woman wrapped in a sheer black sari and nothing else. Anca pulled Derya with her as she danced away from them, guessing they wouldn't be welcome soon. Realizing she was thirsty, she made her way to the bar where she saw a familiar face.

"Hey Ode. You look fabulous." She was wearing a long sleeve backless dress of red lace.

"Thank you. You don't look too bad yourself Derya. Welcome to the world of vampires. Any sign of your man love?" Ode asked Anca.

"No," said Anca looking around for him for the first time. A great plume of flame danced over the heads of the party goers. When it faded, Anca saw Marcial on a balcony, absentmindedly stroking a smaller dragon as he spoke one of The Ancients, Robyn.

Robyn was wearing a collar of upright feathers. Feathers covered her shoulders in delicate, yet commanding epaulettes. Her box braids were half up in a braided crown, the rest fell past her waist. When she wiped blood from her mouth Anca saw she wore bracelets of feathers as well.

Feathers, that's The Ancients' thing this year.

Anca grabbed a drink and made her way to the balcony. Derya was asking Ode a dizzying number of questions about The Gathering and what she should or shouldn't do. Anca had tried to tell her that the rules here were pretty few, but Derya hadn't believed her. "There's no way I'm allowed to feed on any human I see. That's ridiculous." They wouldn't miss Anca.

Anca scanned the room once more. *Not here. Tomorrow maybe.*

She was too distracted to look for Nuru properly. She had some questions for Marcial. His grin faltered when he saw her climb the stairs. She tried to relax her face. *He made a request. You can't rip his throat out for that.* Robyn turned to see what had caused Marcial's smile to fade.

"Anca! It has been a long time." Robyn gave Anca a one-armed hug.

"Anca." Barely five feet tall but emitting a self-imposed power was Kali. She was the oldest vampire that wasn't an Ancient. Her and Veia had never gotten along well.

Kali took a pull from her cigarette holder, the end of the cigarette glowing. "How is retirement?"

"Peaceful."

"Boring?"

Anca turned her attention to Robyn. "How are you? I hear there's a big announcement?"

"You'll have to wait like everyone else. You'll have to give my luck to Trig if I don't see him. I am excited to see what his investments will produce."

"For the blood substitute?" asked Anca.

"Asking us to live off second rate nourishment is insulting. You don't feed a dragon cabbage," said Marcial, stroking the dragon lazing on the rail. It roared a small plume of fire.

"It won't be second rate." Trig joined them on the balcony. "I heard you say my name." He gave Robyn a kiss on the cheek.

"Such promises." Kali blew out a mouthful of smoke.

"Guarantees. I've already found several labs worth our money. Two could have a viable substitute within a year," said Trig.

"So soon?" Kali said. Anca thought her voice seemed a bit strained. Marcial paused his stroking.

"I may have done some research before the council meeting," said Trig with a smile.

"Fake blood is fake blood. We should drink the best as we will and nothing less," said Marcial.

"And bleed the world dry? How would that help keep us hidden?" demanded Anca.

"Why must we stay hidden?" asked Kali.

"Do you remember the witch trials?" asked Anca.

"Times are changing Anca. Humans aren't the only ones that have evolved," Kali drew in a mouthful of smoke.

Marcial's mouth tightened.

Kali gave a dainty exhale allowing the smoke to curl infront of her eyes. "Marcial, I think you and I should get something to eat." She looked at him lazily. Marcial bowed his head slightly. He turned crisply then strode off.

"I feel the need for *human* blood." Kali bared her fangs in a wide, forced smile before following after Marcial.

Anca sipped her drink and shook her head. She peeked over at the bar to check on Derya. She was still talking to Ode, but now there was also a small group of men around them. A dark-skinned beauty wearing a turban seemed to have most of Darya's attention.

"How is Derya adjusting?" asked Robyn.

"Well. She seems anxious to start her studies," said Anca. "Qamar has been guiding her well, but I wanted her to have fun today. Experience being a vampire to the fullest."

"Mission accomplished." Trig pointed. Derya was laughing after having sloshed her drink on one of her admirers.

"Doesn't look like I'll have to punch anyone." Anca felt protective of Derya. If any of those men made a wrong move…

"Ode has her well taken care of. We take care of our young. We all know how precious they are. That's part of what makes your work so important." Robyn turned to Trig. "I and others think our days in the shadows are numbered. When our existence does come to light, we'd like to be able to assure humans we don't just see them as food. We were hunted to near extinction once, and none of us care to have that happen again."

Anca and Derya danced the day away, with Lita disappearing every couple hours with the woman she'd met earlier. Every time she took off, Derya gave Anca a scandalized look. "Are all vampires that… free?"

Anca laughed. "Not most." She pointed at a couple that had just returned. They parted hands and immediately found new partners. "But some. Robyn for example. She and Eubule have been together for over six thousand years."

"Wow." Derya's eyes sparkled.

"You could find that kind of love too. It may take centuries," Anca warned.

"What about you? Why aren't you with anyone?" The question was bold, but Anca wasn't offended. They'd both had more than a few drinks, and Anca insisted on an unfiltered dialogue between them. She had seen vampires make assumptions instead of asking about certain aspects of vampire life: the results could get unpleasant.

"Assumptions. He made some assumptions about what I would do with my life. I didn't let him explain enough. There was fault on both sides." She shrugged.

"I hope things work out."

"Me too."

Derya left not long after. The day was fading, and Qamar had insisted on having Derya for the Day of Mourning. Anca took her leaving as her own signal. She should get ready too. She left the party, giving it one last look. *Tomorrow I'll find him*, she promised herself.

CHAPTER 8

The second day of The Gathering was for remembering. Anca dressed in her room. Her dress was a traditional Romanian dress done in all white, one of the more ancient colors for mourning. She fixed her head piece to her hair with bobby pins, a wonderful invention. A small veil fell back over her hair. She took in her appearance. She wore a straight skirt and short vest both heavily embroidered. Her undershirt had voluminous sleeves, again embroidered, but lightly.

She went to Lita's suite in the newest wing of the castle. Lita always wanted to approve Anca's outfits although Anca knew in part Lita wanted an opinion on her own. "Thank God I've no idea what to wear," said Lita as way of greeting. She left the door open when she retreated into her chic suite. There was a gas fireplace with silver pebbles on the bottom framed in white marble. There was a small bar area with clear barstools and porcelain glassware. The bed was hidden, but Anca knew from her previous visits it was hung from the ceiling by white ropes, very Lita.

"Alright, what do we have to work with?"

As usual Lita had packed about four times as many clothes as she needed. She was staring at five options ranging from modest dress to grand gown to just down right scandalous. "Not this one." Anca took down the sheer mini dress.

"You sure?"

"Definitely. We're trying to be respectful, not get laid."

"Why not both?" Lita looked at the discarded dress.

Anca raised her eyebrows at her.

"Fine." Lita turned back to the dresses then looked at Anca properly for the first time. "You look very respectable."

"Thank you." Anca looked at their choices critically. "You want a gown. I know you want something eye catching so that eliminates this one." She removed another dress. "You want something grand so not quite this one." She pulled down a sleek dress that didn't have any flare. "How about now? Can you make a decision?"

Lita stared at the two dresses. One was a strapless sweetheart neckline covered in crystals the other was a chic off the shoulder gown with a sheer floor length cape. "Respectful..." Lita muttered to herself. She picked up the second dress. "This one." she said confidently.

"Perfect. I'll help you zip." Lita put on a simple face of makeup and styled her hair in romantic curls. They looked at themselves in a large full-length mirror after they were both dressed.

"The old and the new," said Lita.

"Part of what makes us great," said Anca. She elbowed Lita gently, they smiled.

The Second day's celebration took place in the largest hall of the castle. At six stories tall it had dozens of balconies. There were three stained glass windows; each could put any but the grandest churches to shame, but they were covered in red velvet curtains to keep the sunlight off the younger vampires. Everyone observed today, it was unofficially mandatory. With such large windows, the place didn't have as many chandeliers as you might expect, so the whole room was a bit dim adding to the feel of reverie. It did have a grand staircase, it began in two then merged as it went down. The numerous guests were staring at it.

Everyone was dressed in all white, making the hall look like a giant puddle of spilled milk. As for the hall itself, its usual black and gold was covered in red drapes to represent the blood that had been spilled. The contrast was marvelous.

The mother would begin this year's day of mourning. This year, all of the dozens of ancients were present. Anca counted near forty. She hadn't thought so many were still alive. *Maybe I've isolated myself too much lately*. They stood at the top of the stairs all dressed magnificently in white. Most wore crowns or other grand headpieces. Anca thought they looked rather regale until she saw Veia. She was positively alluring.

She was a vision of sparkling elegance. Her gown showed off her figure while still being modest. Large sheer bell sleeves made her look commanding and delicate. Her head was framed by a sprawling Elizabethan collar that shone with crystals and stood a good two feet higher than her head.

"My children."

Silence fell.

"From this moment until next sundown, we mourn the fallen. From the last gathering to this, too many have fallen prey to the eternal sleep. We honor the fallen." She raised a chalice that was handed to her. "May we see them again when the moon is ever risen."

"When the moon is ever risen!" they chorused. Anca saw two moon priestesses mutter their own additional prayer before sipping from their chalices. No blood would be drunk today. The glasses being passed around contained wine or champagne. Vampires could eat human food, but only drinking blood regularly maintained their strength. This would be a taxing day.

Like most things, this inconvenience had more of an effect on younger vampires or vampires that weren't used to the practice. Anca turned down any more drink; drinking on an empty stomach wasn't a good idea even if you were undead. Nate nodded to her as he passed. He was one of the vampires that took the fasting more seriously. Nate probably hadn't had any blood for hours already. Anca wondered if that made the food prep he did harder or if he was so practiced at it like her that it didn't bother him anymore.

The day consisted of what were basically eulogies. There was a small memorial for each vampire that had died in the last fifty years. At each, one vampire after another stepped up and told fond memories of the vampire represented. Among the remembered was two Ancients and one trueborn vampire. It had been quite the shock. They had all been found within months of each other fourteen years ago. She visited each one's memorial.

Anca hated this part. She understood its importance, though. Vampires outlived any humans that would remember them; this was what they would all eventually leave behind. After hours of listening to laughter, crying, and endless stories, it was night. They all filed down to the crypts for the final step of mourning.

There were multiple crypts around the world, but as The Gathering was here they toured this one. As with everything else in this castle, it was massive. Where the tallest room inside the castle was four stories high, the crypt went down seven, with no floors to block the view. When more room was needed, they either dug deeper or created a room off the main staircase. Some vampires requested they be buried as families. A few vampires broke from the single file line to acknowledge their future plot. Each vampire touched every headstone as they passed in recognition of the life that was, polishing the headstones. The process took hours.

Mourning began at sundown and ended at the next sunrise. Thirty-two hours with no blood. Anca was just starting to feel it at the end. She had run missions in the past where she had to go without blood for two days. Animal blood could substitute, but it wasn't the same.

Trig stood next to her. "Gods I'm hungry."

"We've dealt with worse," said Anca.

"Most of them haven't. They look as though they're ready to keel over." He looked at a newly turned vampire. He looked famished. He also looked drunk. He'd been downing champagne left and right as a substitute for blood.

"Oh, that poor guy," said Nuru.

Anca spun around. He was wearing a silk vest over a collared shirt. His tie was white paisley with a mother of pearl clip. The white contrasted against his dark skin in such a way that made him look imposing and beautiful at the same time.

"Very traditional." He gave Anca an appreciative look.

"Oh, look Sarah." Trig left.

"Subtle," Anca muttered.

"I saw you at the jousting," Nuru said.

"I didn't see you."

"Well I saw you. I saw a lot of you."

She blushed. She caught a glimpse of Lita over Nuru's shoulder. She gave her a look that said, *If you don't flirt, I will hurt you.*

"Did- did you compete?"

"You know I didn't. Why were you wearing that dress?" He looked like he knew.

Veia's voice rang throughout the hall. "My children the sun rises and so with it our spirits. Our mourning may end and with it our fasting." She nodded. Humans emerged from behind pillars. They wore dresses that were descending rings of champagne flutes filled with blood. Nuru took a glass and sipped it slowly, watching Anca.

Anca took a swig before taking a steadying breath. "I think you know."

"I've missed you," Nuru said. His eyes locked on her.

"I've missed you too."

"So then…" He leaned forward. Anca didn't move. At the last second, she tipped her head up, meeting his lips with her own. Just as they finally touched, after so many years apart, so many wasted years -- *the east wall exploded.*

CHAPTER 9

Anca felt a wave of energy pass through her. Nuru's eyes were glowing an unnatural shade of gold. His power must have grown significantly in their years apart. Her arms were raised to protect herself from the falling rubble but they weren't needed, Nuru was somehow blocking it. No, not Nuru. One of The Ancients. Briton's chubby face was twisted in concentration. Anca looked around, none of the rubble was moving. Another Ancient tapped Briton's shoulder, all of the rubble fell at once smashing against invisible bubbles of protection around each vampire and human. Glass showered the dance floor from the priceless stained-glass windows.

Vampires and feeders scattered to the cover that could be found under the balconies. Anca saw a vampire she didn't know escorting The Ancients away from the danger. Cans of what smelled like sleeping gas showered from every opening. Everywhere feeders began coughing. *Too hard*, Anca quickly realized. The tear gas was magnified for vampires: it would kill the humans. Others were realizing the same. Anca saw Lita running away with numerous feeders in toe. A wind blew through the room carrying most of the poison out of the hole in the wall. Anca saw Robyn's face twisted in concentration. She'd specialized in air manipulation with her eternity but creating wind indoors didn't happen without effort.

Soldiers in full riot gear and gas masks swarmed in from every direction. *Every direction?* They must have been inside, Anca realized. She cursed the lack of indoor cameras. She pushed aside the thought. Younger vampires were starting to feel the effects of the gas. Anca grabbed two daggers from a display on the wall.

She stood for a moment daggers in hand. She'd spent the last few hundred years avoiding violence. Did she really want to jump back into this? She saw a bullet hit the wall next to Lita. That was all Anca needed, *no one* messed with Lita. Not while she Anca still had blood in her veins.

"Cover me." She told Nuru. She felt an energy pass around her. Nuru was making her invisible to any human that wasn't specifically looking for her. Unless she touched someone, they wouldn't know she was there.

The first soldier didn't even have his gun raised fully. His throat accepted her dagger like warmed butter. The blood sprayed her carefully picked dress. She couldn't care less, didn't even register the mess: she was already eviscerating her next target. His guts spilled onto the floor. His screams were background noise to the crunch of a humerus and then spinal cord.

She hadn't fought to kill in years. She hadn't forgotten a thing. She dodged flying ruble as she attacked. In the time it took a human to blink, near a dozen soldiers had fallen at her hands. And she hadn't even started. Her daggers were a mercy. If Anca had been unarmed she would have simply started tearing off limbs. Armor or no armor, these men didn't stand a chance. They were beginning to realize it too.

She felt the energy Nuru had been projecting fade. She looked behind her to see him caught up in his own fight. She threw one of her daggers at the man attacking him. Trusting he'd be able to take care of himself, she turned back to her task of killing as many of those assholes as she could pushing aside her gnawing hunger.

A voice rang in her head. *Flash bomb in three, two, one.* She slammed her eyes shut. Her vision went from black, to red, to pale pink as one of the magick users created a blinding flash of light. She heard the humans scream. Some of them were probably permanently blinded. They fell to her remaining dagger.

Around her, the attacking humans were being sliced down. Sprays of blood erupted as hearts were torn out and throats sliced open. The witches had gathered together. Their chanting was growing louder and more frantic. She watched bullets fall useless in a circle around them. Any human that got within ten feet of them started bleeding from their eyes. Vampires started gathering around them, hiding within their protective circle. Briton and Robyn had stayed behind, they were overlooking the attack helping as they could. Briton was throwing ruble at anything that looked suspicious, Robyn was sucking air away from the faces of the attackers so they suffocated where they stood. Both of their faces were contorted with the effort.

Anca didn't go toward the circle. She wasn't one to hide. She slammed an elbow into a throat, crushing it. The attacker flailed at her face, ripping off her veil. She threw a knife at an attacking human. The knife sunk deep but the attacker didn't slow. *He's not human.*

What the fuck?

Adjusting her maneuvers, she simply accepted the new truth that some of the attackers were vampires and pushed it to the 'question it later' part of her mind.

"Anca!" Trig threw a sword to her. She didn't question how he'd gotten it. She grabbed it, spun away from the bullets the attacker was shooting and cut him in half then spun and chopped off his head in a blink. She ripped out his heart letting it slap onto the ground not giving it a backward glance as she threw the sword back to Trig with a nod of thanks.

The flow of attack was starting to slow. It would have given some solace except that all around more and more vampires were succumbing to the gas. The youngest vampires were dancing the edge of consciousness. *Our population is so young, so vulnerable. And we're weakened from the fasting. How did they know?* Why hadn't she thought of it before? They had been so focused on regrowing their ranks that they'd barely given a thought to the fact that those of their population under two hundred years old, over half, were a liability against a strategic enemy.

That was certainly what was happening. Anca was just beginning to realize just how lethal their enemy was. She had killed dozens yes but bullets rained from everywhere and nowhere. *Snipers.*

A head shot wouldn't kill vampires over a century but the younger ones... Anca snapped her head around looking for the source of a scream she had hoped she would never hear. Hada held her sister. She was releasing such a shattering scream of sorrow Anca thought her bones would give out.

At first, she thought Janelle was merely hurt. Until she noticed that the pool of red circling her head was slowly growing. It wasn't just her hair. The laughter in her eyes had gone.

In the space of a heartbeat, Anca looked at the wound she now saw just above Janelle's hairline. The angle of the entry, had she fallen straight down...

Anca's eyes snapped up locking with that of the sniper's through the lingering smoke. He had long enough for his expression to change from confusion to horror as Anca picked up a rifle from a fallen soldier, aim, and fire. She killed him on the first shot. She kept firing, walking, screaming, toward the corpse, the *vermin*, that could have taken such a pure life. She didn't stop until the clip was empty. She was about to look for another rifle when the body fell.

A hail of bullets hit her in the back, shoulder, leg, one grazed her head. She bounded on all fours toward her attacker. She wasn't fazed: she was pissed. She didn't have her daggers anymore. Limb ripping it was.

She started with the fucker's head. A second soldier tried to take up the task of attacking her. She nearly laughed at how easy his arm came off. She wasn't encountering any vampire attackers anymore. Anca felt uneasy.

She turned to see Trig snap a soldier's neck and toss him onto a small pile of corpses he had created. The body fell short. He was starting to fatigue. *So am I.* Anca realized. The attack had happened at the worst possible time. Everywhere she looked vampires were struggling to fight. There wasn't time to feed on the attackers; they were getting weaker.

Just as she was beginning to lose hope, the attacks slowed. Lita came sprinting back into the room through the haze. She lifted her chin to Anca. She shrugged. There were no more soldiers. Why?

Unease settled over her. She'd never gotten the hang of magick. But gut instinct was something everyone had.

She scanned the room. Corpses, only corpses and vampires. Why had they stopped? Were they out of men? Why bother with a siege if you weren't able to see it through?

"I don't like this," she said.

"Me neither," said Trig. He too was scanning.

She picked up one of the cans. It was custom made. What gave her pause was what she found when she turned it over. A second canister. As if someone had been watching, every can went off a second time. This gas was different, it *burned*. How could it burn? How could it burn her? She looked at Trig in panic. He was younger than her. He was bent double, coughing. Soon Anca was on her knees trying not to cough up a lung. *What was this?*

She saw feet approaching. *Fucking idiots.* She killed two despite her condition. The only reason she stopped (she would have kept going even if she did cough up a lung) was a knife going through her cervical spine.

CHAPTER 10

Anca woke up in a lab. *A lab?* She took in every detail, her confusion turning to focus, then pure unbridled fury. *What had happened?*

Urian was next to her strapped to an examination chair. His eyes fluttered. He was alive.

"Urian?"

His eyes opened. "Yeah?"

"Thank God."

"Hmm?"

Anca looked around some more. She saw a mirror directly in front of them. In its reflection she read the label on the glass door behind them. Non Ancient. Nonskilled Magic Users.

So, they know neither of us are Ancients and they know that neither of us are that great at magick. That means we have a mole. Great.

It explained why the attack was so well timed. Vampires were weakest when they haven't fed in a while. They had just been breaking their fast when the attack happened. They had hit them at their absolute weakest. More evidence that they had someone on the inside.

Someone who?

She filed that question away too. Judging by how hungry she was, the attack had been less than a day ago. They could be anywhere in the world with that time frame. She thought of Nuru, Lita, Trig. She prayed they were okay.

I thought jumping back into fighting would have been harder. When I saw my family in danger though… I don't care how much I want peace, no one hurts my family and lives.

A quiet swoosh of electric doors got Anca's attention. She watched the mirror. A man in a white lab coat entered the room.

"Awake at last?"

"How long were we out?" She feigned confusion. She knew how long she had been out. *What kept me out for so long?* Panic threatened to enter her mind. She refused it entry. There was no way she and Urian were the only ones captured. The others might be in better condition, but they could also be in far worse condition.

She took stock of her restraints. Heavy metal encircled her wrists (which were forced behind her back), knees, ankles, and circled her head like a crown. *What are they planning on doing to us? What is happening to the others?*

"Oh, not too long." The man made a note on his clipboard. Right handed, swirly yet messy handwriting. Pair that with the obviously inflated ego and the circumstances and Anca put two and two together quickly. Doctor.

"Where are we?" asked Urian.

"In our care," said the doctor.

"What'd you drug us with?" asked Anca.

"Just a cocktail of ours." He looked at some monitors.

An organization. One with money, one that knew about vampires, one that was smart enough to attack them with medicine. *Shit.*

If they others had been woken up sooner they could already be being experimented on. Anca's stomach rolled at the thought.

She fought to keep her voice even. "Including…?"

"Nothing you need worry about. There won't be any long-term effects."

These were the people kidnapping werewolves I know it. They must be responsible for the missing Ancients too. They'd need subjects to test their cocktail on to know it didn't have long-term effects. She thought about the two Ancients everyone thought had gone on holiday. Perhaps they had been captured as well. *Are they still here?*

"Fuck you," Anca growled.

"Now, now, there is no need to get hostile."

"Says the man helping the people that just blew up a family reunion. Get bent."

He glanced at the small mirror on the wall. They were being watched. She had assumed. If the mirror was a one way with a room on the other side, she could break through and escape.

"How many of us did you capture?"

"Enough."

"Please be more vague; it thrills me."

"You have quite the attitude." He chuckled as he made a note on the clipboard.

"I also have quite the appetite." She bared her fangs at him.

He swallowed. His apparent fear gave her a moment of satisfaction. Walking to a panel on the wall he pressed a button. "Could I get extra restraints in here?"

Pussy.

A moment later a guard walked in. Bullet proof vest, handgun, two dirks strapped across his back. He carried a length of chain. *Fucking idiots*, she thought as he wrapped the chain around her. They'd just given her a possible weapon. The guard left after she'd been wrapped up.

"So… Doc," she raised her eyebrows sarcastically. "What are we in for? Ran out of bunny rabbits to test mascara on?"

"You are here to be studied." He approached Urian with an empty syringe. He plugged in a vial and filled it.

"What about us are you studying?" she asked. *What is happening to the others?*

"Take a guess." He filled a few vials with Urian's blood; then he approached Anca. She considered her options. If she started breaking free, this coward wouldn't draw her blood, and it wouldn't be used for whatever heinous thing they wanted it for. But if she did that, she couldn't continue to interrogate this doctor. He was giving her everything.

She felt the restraints around her wrists cool significantly. She looked at Urian out of the corner of her eye. His eyes were closed in concentration. She tried to lend what little skill she had to his efforts chilling the restraints. She had to keep the doctor distracted.

"Why do you care about our blood?"

"Your virus is quite the puzzle. How it attaches to the host, how it changes your DNA… We still don't know everything about it."

"But why me specifically? Why not just kill me?"

Her concentration had broken. She wasn't helping chill the restraints anymore. She felt them warm up. They were hot, very hot. She tried not to wriggle.

"You're old." He shrugged. They had abducted The Ancients, she was sure of it. "The virus in your veins hasn't morphed as much as others. It hasn't evolved as much. You were turned by an Ancient so your virus is closer to the original More pure." He plugged in a vial. It quickly filled with her blood.

That explained why they had attacked The Gathering. Every Ancient had been there. That's what Trig had said. Some big announcement that they had never got around to making. What was it? If they knew about Ancients, knew about The Gathering, knew about how the virus was purer in older vampires… She thought about the vampire she hadn't recognized escorting The Ancients away. *Shit.*

So, they've been studying the vampire virus for some time then. She thought about The Ancients that had supposedly gone on holiday. *They must have captured them for study. They must not have them anymore if they needed new subjects. They still have questions.* They wanted to know how the virus changed their DNA. Vampires had known they were vampires because of some virus for decades now. They too, had recently discovered it altered their DNA. It hadn't been that hard to puzzle out before the official results came in. They were permanently changed after being infected. Of course, their DNA was altered. But why did these people care, unless...

"You want to become vampires without dying," she said. Her restraints started to cool once more.

"Of course not." There was disdain there.

Ironic attitude for someone willing to destroy a family. "You're trying to splice the virus with something else then."

"Something like that." He still thought he was the smartest person in the room. He put down the second vial of her blood and plugged in a third. The blood surged into the tube.

"Splice it with what? Why? If you don't want to become vampires-"

"Stop talking to the subject," said a voice over the intercom.

Holy shit.

She wasn't thrown by the voice. She knew they'd be interrupted eventually. If they were splicing their virus with something else but not for their own use… Soldiers, they were making soldiers.

The doctor returned to his clipboard. Anca made a few more attempts to talk to him. He didn't say a word. He pulled a tray toward her. It was covered in various syringes. Each was filled with something different.

"What's that for?"

"The bunny rabbit." He smiled as he picked up his first syringe.

"Proud of that joke, are you?" Anca said deadpan.

His smile faltered. He squirted out some of the liquid, tapping the side of the syringe. He started toward her.

"Fuck that." She pulled at her restraints. They were hard, harder than she'd expected. Steel would have yielded easier. *Perhaps it is lined with titanium?* Urian had managed to weaken the material by freezing and thawing it repeatedly.

The doctor froze, terror on his face. "How?" he muttered.

This is taking longer than I'd like. Steel she could have snapped instantly, this took several seconds. The doctor froze in fear, then ran for the door. The door remained shut. He slammed the flat of his hands on the doors, screaming for help.

Her hands were free. She freed her head, then knees. Kicking her legs out she snapped the metal around her ankles. The chain fell lamely to the floor.

Taking her time, she approached the doctor. "What about this job made you think it was a good idea?"

He whimpered, sinking to the floor.

"You're going to die for what was done to my family. And then I'm going to kill every one of your employers. Who are they?" Her voice was quiet, deadly. She was the calm before the storm. No, she was the eye of the storm. That quiet that when it hits, you know you're fucked.

"I, I, I…" His mumbling was pathetic.

"You better tell me who you work for. What company owns this building?"

"Not… not a company."

"Then who?" Her patience was straining.

He managed to get out a single word. "Church."

"What church?"

"Light. Heaven."

"WHAT CHURCH!"

"Church of -- Church of Heavenly Light."

Seriously? How cheesy. "How many companies do they own? Which ones?"

He shook his head, mumbling. He didn't know.

"What is happening to the others that were taken?"

"Punish… Please. Tests…" He was sobbing.

Oh, you'll be punished. You'll all be punished.

"What else do you know about your employers? Is this the only lab?"

Again, he shook his head. There were multiple labs.

"Where are the other labs?"

Again, he shook his head. He began to wet himself. *Great*. He wouldn't tell her anything else. He was useless now.

She bent down. He tried to back up but was blocked by the door.

"Shh, shh. It will be qui-" She snapped his neck.

She went over to Urian. His restraints were cold to the touch. "Keep cool." She hoped he understood. If someone was watching she didn't want them to figure out how they were escaping. Urian understood her, the restraints were freezing. She snapped the bonds around his wrists and around his head. With great effort he broke the rest.

Scanning the room, she looked for anything that might be helpful in figuring out what was going on here. She took the doctor's clipboard. Enlightened Genetics Corp. was watermarked at the top of the paper. She checked for more paperwork, nothing. She tore off the paper and stuffed it in her bra. She was still wearing her dress and it didn't have pockets.

The door opened.

"Watch out!" cried Urian.

Anca grabbed the chain that had been wrapped around her, then whipped the incoming guard. His head snapped around. He was looking directly behind himself. *Human then*. He fell to the floor. The door closed behind him.

She whipped the chain through the mirror. Urian threw his hands up to protect his face from the raining glass. She launched through the jagged opening. The space was empty. She heard a set of doors shut just beyond the ones she could see. She'd just missed them. Anca found herself disappointed.

"Clear!"

"Is that good?" asked Urian.

Right, he's not a soldier.

Neither were you until the attack.

I guess you don't stop being a soldier.

"Come on then." Hairline cracks appeared on the door when the heel of her foot made contact with the reinforced glass door. Three more karate front kicks and she was through. No alarm sounded that she could tell. She went back in the room and wrapped the chain around her arm. She gave the doctor a long look. She was starving but something kept her from feeding off the doctor and the guard. Urian lunged at the body. "Don't!"

"I'm starving." He looked desperate.

"They know too much about us, they could have poisoned themselves." He looked from her to the body. With great effort he turned away from the body.

A stark white hallway was beyond the door. She looked at the label to the side of the door she had just come through. These rooms weren't just fitted for vampires they were fitted for different kinds of vampires. They knew The Ancients were stronger but didn't realize an Elder like Anca was stronger than a new vampire. *Thank the Gods.* If they had put her in a room fitted for an Ancient there's no way she would have been able to get out.

She looked at Urian. "You okay?"

"Tired, hungry." He looked unsteady. He wasn't close to being a soldier. Urian was meant to woo women and recite poetry, not to withstand two days of fasting and exhausting magick use.

"I'm getting us out of here but need to find whoever we can first," said Anca.

He nodded.

A patrolling guard, gun raised, rounded the nearby corner. She ducked just in time. He was a good shot. He recovered quickly, too quickly, and fired at Urian, hitting him in the stomach. A cloud of blue smoke circled the guard's head. He swatted at it frantically, Urian's face twisted in pain and determination. Anca used the opening Urian had given her to attack the guard. He yelled as he brought his handgun down, trying to pistol whip her, baring his fangs. *Fangs?* He was a vampire, a vampire working for the lab.

What the hell?

She dodged the attack leaping up. Wrapping her left leg around the back of his head she used her momentum to slam him to the ground. He fell supine on the floor. He barely had time to yell before she brought her heel to his neck. That didn't kill him. It is extremely hard to kill a vampire.

She ripped off his head and tore out his heart leaving him in pieces. The blue smoke cleared. Finally, she had a moment to think. "Which way should we go?" she asked not really expecting an answer.

Urian shrugged, clutching his stomach.

"Shit." She tore off her vest and pressed it to his abdomen.

"I'll heal."

"Yeah, and the bullet will be stuck in there. It will be uncomfortable believe me."

They looked at the hole pouring blood. Urian had precious little to spare, he was getting weaker by the second. "Maybe I can try cauterizing it." Urian raised his finger making to touch the wound.

Anca grabbed his wrist. "Magick takes energy. You should put yours into getting out of here, getting to help." Urian let his hand fall to his side, nodding, blinking slowly. She had to get them out of there.

Closing her eyes, she listened. The buzz of electric lightbulbs, the hollow echo of an empty hallway. She smelled, the tang of bleach, the echo of human sweat, and... blood. The faintest note of blood. She turned left, toward the smell, sprinting. She found Lita, ripping out a guard's neck with her bare hands. A doctor lay dead, used as a battering ram, halfway through a glass door just like Anca and Urian's room.

"You're alive!" Relief flooded Lita's voice.

Anca ran into her arms.

"I'm fine. Did they do anything to you?" Asked Anca.

Lita looked from Anca to Urian. "They just tried to take some blood. There was a tray of syringes, but I wasn't about to let that happen," said Lita

"Same," said Anca. She looked over Urian's shoulder. Video cameras. She grabbed the pistol from the still thrashing guard and fired.

"Good idea." said Lita. She ran back into the room. She came back out with a small bag that clinked of glass. She'd grabbed the syringes they would have been stuck with. "We need to know what they're up to."

"Good idea." Anca had been so preoccupied with *who* was doing this she'd forgotten to try and figure out *why* they were doing this. Why did they want soldiers? They sprinted down the hall to find the others.

"You were alone?" asked Anca.

"No, Derya was with me. I told her to find help. We should catch up with her soon."

In a moment they saw Derya. She was standing still staring at a lab door. A look of horror was on her face. The label on the door read Non Ancient Threat.

Anca pulled up short. Inside she saw Trig drugged out. He was sluggishly trying to fight off a guard. His movements were slow and weak, even by human standards. She froze. Horror swept her mind, blocking out everything else. Even Lita's voice.

"What is he --? Oh my God."

Trig was bent over a table. The guard was behind him. Raping him.

CHAPTER 11

Anca had never felt such a cold permeate her before. She didn't think about her long ago promise to keep out of violence. She didn't think about how sore she was. All her focus was on the man that was harming, defiling, her son.

She kicked in the door, shattering it on her fist kick. The guard looked up in shock. She slammed her arm into his throat but not with enough force to crush it, even though she could. Instead she pinned him to the wall. Anca was unaware that her appearance had changed. Her eyes had darkened, black on red. The man looked into those eyes and saw nothing but cruelty and hatred. She bore into him with her stare. Slowly she picked the guard's knife out of his belt. Showed it to him, then carefully, and oh so slowly, cut across his abdomen.

She made sure not to cut too high -- that would cause his diaphragm to collapse, killing him much too quickly. She made sure not to cut too deep -- that would kill him too quickly too. Instead she cut about one inch below the ribs in a slightly downward curved line. Her gaze never warmed, never wavered. The man screamed. He tried to wiggle his way free. She pressed herself against one of his legs, limiting his movement. When the cut was complete she pointed at Trig with the knife.

"You violated my son." Her voice was low, guttural, savage, cold enough to freeze fire. Behind her, Lita helped Trig get his pants on. He was limp, exhausted from the assault and the drugs. She looked at Anca with fear in her eyes. "Never piss off a mother." Anca plunged her hands into the man's guts. She felt the organs slide against her arms. Her sleeves were pushed up a bit. His screams would have deafened a human. "Because it will be the last thing you do. Rapist." She spat the word, pulled his intestines out, foot by foot. She could feel the connective tissue snapping. The rest of his organs followed. The man was beyond screaming then. She let him fall to the floor, her breathing heavy.

At last she looked at Trig. Tears streamed down his face. "Mom," he whimpered. He'd only ever called her that in his deepest moments of sorrow. Not since they watched the witches burn had he called her that. She knelt on the floor pulling him into her arms. Blood smeared into his blond hair. She looked at Lita. Her face had turned hard. She nodded. What Anca had done was cruel but justified.

"We need to leave," Lita said gently. "We need to find the others."

Anca could see Urian holding a weeping Derya in the hallway, red splotches of blood leaching across their white formal wear. Innocents stained. She had become a vampire so she could learn. This wasn't something Anca had wanted her to learn.

"Can you walk?" she asked Trig.

"I'm getting there," he said weakly.

"He had a drip. He should recover quickly now that it's out." Lita whispered. Anca could tell she was trying to stay cold. They all needed to keep themselves detached from what they might have to do to get out of here.

Anca looked behind her to the mass of organs whimpering on the floor. He had kept her son on a sedative drip so he could... Rage threatened to flood her senses. She forced herself to look at Lita, whose face was calm. Somehow Lita was able to turn herself to stone in these kinds of situations. Anca thought of her as her anchor. "We need to get the others," she said, reminding Anca that they had to leave.

Anca nodded, lifting Trig over her shoulder without a word. He slid slightly against her slickened arms. She wiped them on her dress. Without a backwards glance, she carried him out of the room.

Each room they came across held a new horror. Most were relatively unscathed, but others had been experimented on. One younger vampire had had his hand cut off and then sewn back on: it wasn't clear if it would heal. They'd emptied near a dozen rooms, over twenty vampires, when a small group of guards barreled down the hall at them. Anca shoved down her rising panic. Trig was still too groggy to be of much benefit in a fight. She heard Derya behind her. She set down Trig next to her. "Watch each other." Anca squared her shoulders and faced the guards armed with guns and machetes. She held her chain at the ready.

Urian stared at the oncoming guards. A giant white bear covered in feathers appeared. It roared at the attackers before running at them. The guards fired as they ran and slowed down for a moment when they saw the bear. The moment they were within reach of the bear they realized it was only an illusion and ignored it. Urian collapsed in exhaustion, and the bear disappeared.

Another vampire took his place, electricity sparking at her fingers. The guards were covered in blood. After a moment one ran out of ammunition and threw the rifle aside. *They fought the others not long ago.*

The vampire with electricity dancing at her fingers ran forward. She rolled between the guards then stood up behind them grabbing two by the neck. They went rigid and passed out. *Human, good.*

Anca stepped forward, Lita at her side. They dodged the bullets fired at them. Lita grabbed a rifle from one of the guards and used it against the rest. Anca swung the chain low, breaking the legs of the humans. She swung it higher and heard the crack of a face breaking.

"Anca!" The vampire using her electricity as a weapon gestured for the chain. Anca threw it. The woman grabbed it, wrapped it around a few guards and used the chain as a conductor. Several guards fell victim to her at once.

Anca saw a guard go for Trig. Derya was next to him, each trying to protect the other. Trig pushed her out of the way leaving himself exposed. Anca dove for the guard and put her fist through his chest. She heard the footsteps of another guard approach her and a bullet whistle past her head, she turned to face him. She saw Derya not a foot from her. She had broken the guard's neck, but not before he had stabbed her through the heart with his machete and taken a bullet to the side of her head.

Derya dropped the guard. Her hands went to the handle sticking out of her chest. Blood poured down both sides of her white dress. She turned toward Anca.

She's too young. Anca knew that wound on a vampire as young as Derya wouldn't heal, not in time.

Derya's face paled as she watched her life pump out of her. "But --" Derya fell sideways, a confused look on her face.

Trig looked from Derya to Anca in horror.

Anca wanted to break more necks, kill more of the guards but when she looked up she saw the last of the guards fall victim to the chain. Smoke rose from their bodies as they convulsed. They hit the floor. Everyone was silent.

"No." Lita kneeled next to Anca. "No, she can't."

"Derya?" Trig limped forward. He touched Derya's neck. His face hardened and then he closed his eyes.

Lita carefuly lifted Derya's body. "We need to find the others," she sobbed. Tears began to fall down her cheeks. They nodded, what else could they do? Staying there wouldn't bring Derya back to life and each moment they waited could cause another of their family to die.

They quickly chopped off heads and ripped out hearts. They couldn't have these guards following them. Anca had hoped it would feel a bit like revenge, but any time she glanced at Derya's limp form she was reminded there was nothing she could do to bring her back.

Anca draped Trig's arm over her shoulders. They all made their way down the hall. They didn't come in contact with more guards but came across more labs and freed more vampires. The same pattern was found. Individual vampires were experimented on, though they never found anyone else getting humiliated like Trig had been. The experiments dealt with different parts of being a vampire, mostly healing. Hanare was no exception. Trig was walking on his own at that point. He gave a sigh of release when he saw that Hanare hadn't sustained any permanent damage.

Strips of skin were missing, and his jaw was broken but that would heal. Being a younger vampire, he hadn't healed *yet*. As they were helping him out of the chair Isobel came to the shattered door. "Have you seen --" She saw Hanare, the skin missing from his arms, the obvious deformity of his jaw.

There is a state a vampire can enter into, something newer vampires referred to as 'full vamp mode.' It only occurred when a vampire was pushed over the edge, when you saw something that nearly broke your world. Anca was sure she had just experienced it herself when she saw what had happened to Trig. It happened now to Isobel. Sweet Isobel, the living china doll.

Anca watched as the whites of her eyes flood with blood, turning them completely red. Her irises darkened to black. The blood vessels around her eyes swelled slightly. There was no humanity left in her eyes. She turned to the doctor. Irina was questioning him, they had learned a few things about exit locations, number of rooms on each floor and other basics of the building. "Isobel, don't --" she said.

But it was useless. In a single stride she was on him, lifting him up by the neck. With her other hand, she ripped out his heart. She stared at the man until the light went out of his eyes. Limp, he crumpled to the floor when he was released. She looked back at Hanare. She looked like a nightmare.

"Well, I can't say I blame you," said Irina.

Hanare gave a weak chuckle from the chair. Isobel's face flooded with relief, her eyes started to return to normal. If her husband was still capable of laughter that meant she hadn't lost him, he would be okay.

Anca and the others helped those they'd found. The ones who'd been alone in their labs were in rough shape. They'd been separated so they could be experimented on or humiliated. Anca was beginning to decipher the signs on the doors. They'd been sorted according to their threat level. Trig was strong, an Elder that could command respect. He'd been singled out to deflate his ego, ruin his reputation. Anca suspected there was more to it than that but couldn't put her finger on why.

They made their way forward one lab at a time, releasing any vampire and killing every doctor and guard they got their hands on after some interrogation. There were still dozens of vampires missing, and they hadn't seen any sign of an Ancient. Anca knew they must be here somewhere from the sign on her door but had no clue as to where.

And there was another thought pressing on her mind. Why, when these people seemed so well supplied and informed, had they been able to break out? If they knew about the strength of The Ancients and the vulnerability of new vampires why didn't they know of the intermediate strength of the Elders? Of course, if they knew everything they wouldn't have brought them here to be experimented on.

Anca's head kept filling with more questions. She shoved them to the back of her mind. Only two questions mattered right now. Where were the rest of the vampires? How were they going to get out?

Visibly shaken, Goran brought up a disturbing point. "Why'd they attack The Gathering? It is one of our most guarded meetings." His braids were coming out of his bun, his dark skin was paling. They'd tried to drain him of blood. As soon as they'd broken his bonds he'd drained the doctor. Blood was still around his mouth.

"Don't know, don't care right now," said Isobel. "I just want us out of here." She was too busy fretting over Hanare to care about much else.

Four vampires came running from the direction Anca had started from. Hada was among them looking completely defeated. Anca tried not to imagine the girl's pain. She'd watch her twin die in her arms only to be snatched away and experimented on. She was wearing a paper gown. So far anyone wearing a paper gown had been experimented on brutally. Sure enough, Anca noticed Hada was holding her right hand tenderly and had a definite limp. Like her hips were in pain.

"Hada, what…?"

The vampire next to her, Nate the chef, answered Anca's unasked question. "They were drilling into her sacrum. We think they were trying to extract spinal fluid." Nate wasn't that old as far as vampires go -- only a couple hundred years, but somehow he always ended up playing dad to everyone else. He kept an eye on Hada at all times, ready to assist her at a second's notice.

"The Ancients are on another floor," said Victor. Was it only a few days ago Anca had seen him in the garage? "We questioned the guards. We took out three so far." The questioning must have been similar to Anca's.

Victor had abandoned his jacket, and his white shirt was splattered with blood. The combination was both unsettling and a little sexy. *Not the time*, thought Anca. With a pang she remembered that she had no idea where Nuru was. She didn't even know if he had been taken.

"Are all the labs cleared that way?" asked Anca.

"Yes," said Victor. "Ours were at the end. I got out of my chair and took out the doctor. I was about to start on the door when Chance kicked it in. We got Hada then Nate. We passed another lab, but the door was shattered already. The doctor dead and a guard in the hallway. The guard looked like --"

"He was, that was the lab I was in." said Anca. *Another mystery. Why was there a vampire guard here? Why were the rest only human?* It didn't make any sense. Rogue vampires were rare, a scattered minority in the vampire world. Most died shortly after being turned not knowing how to feed without drawing attention, stepping into sunlight without knowing the consequences, or overestimating their strength.

"I guess we move this way then." Meryem had just come from down the hall. Xerxes stood behind her carrying numerous guns. Anca hadn't realized how worried she was about her until she saw she was okay.

"Thank goodness." She pulled her friend into a hug. "You're okay?" Anca touched a cut that was already healing across Meryem's forehead.

"Fine. I hope you're all here swapping intel."

"Sort of. Victor says The Ancients are upstairs."

"We'll get them then. I sent a group off already. They aren't far. Anyone here that isn't up for a fight should catch up with them," said Meryem.

After much protest, Trig, Hada, Nate, Hanare, Urian, and the rest of the injured went to catch up with the ones that had already left.

"I can fight." Trig whispered to Anca. He was steady on his feet; the drug had worked its way out of his system.

"Exactly, someone in that group needs to be able to fight in case you run into anything. Look at them. You've all been through hell. A fighter needs to go with them, give them strength."

Trig nodded, reluctantly accepting the truth of her words. "Mom..." Anca held back tears at the word. "Thank you." His eyes were hard.

"My only regret will be that I didn't let you help." Her voice was low, on the edge of cracking.

Trig gave a sad smile.

"Protect them," said Anca as she nudged his shoulder.

He nodded and then sprinted down the hall.

"Alright, the last magick user just left. They haven't fed in too long they don't have any fight in them, so it is up to us. Let's get our Ancients back," said Meryem. Her tone was more someone stating they were getting groceries than someone who was planning a rescue mission.

Those of them that were still in fighting condition looked ridiculous. Half of them were in paper gowns and half of them were still in their formal wear. All of them were covered in various amounts of blood. Isobel had blood drenching the front of her white silk gown, her necklace of diamonds so covered in blood they looked like rubies. Anca's forearms were completely red, the entire front of her skirt drenched. Lita somehow, only had sparse splatterings of blood.

"How is it," Anca asked her, "that even when we're escaping a death lab, you look the best?"

"Strength of will." Lita said. She'd ripped off the cape portion of her gown. Her shoes bounced against the rifle Xerxes had given her as they made their way up the stairs. "I don't *let* the blood get on me."

Anca held up the pistol that had been given to her, a Beretta M9. There were thirteen rounds left. She still had the chain wrapped around her for when she ran out. The guard that had brought her chains had gone to Chance's room. She held the dirks in a guard position when they stopped. They were outside the door to the floor that supposedly held The Ancients.

Meryem looked back at Anca. Gripping her M4 carbine securely but loosely. "Formation?"

Anca thought a moment. "Bottleneck sweep. Segmented."

Meryem nodded in agreement. She explained the formation to the others. Not all of them were as trained as they were.

Chance nodded in determination. Her soldier background was shining through. All of theirs were. Somehow, they'd gone from party guests, to victims, to fighters in a day.

Anca went to the front of the group, braced herself, and then nodded. Meryem, brought a thumb out of her pocket. It was from one of the guards. A place like this, body parts could come in handy. They were right. She pressed it against a small pad, a tiny light blinked green, the latch clicked open.

They had expected another stark hallway. What was before them looked like a mad science lab mashed with an aquarium. They saw over twenty of The Ancients immediately. Anca's stomach twisted. The Ancients hung suspended in massive tanks that were covered in a confusion of tubes and wires.

The group moved between the tanks. Meryem raised a fist, a sign to halt. Anca watched her inspect the control pad of the tank, trying to figure out how to get The Ancients out. Next to her, a vampire was wearing a paper gown. Together they tried to puzzle out the control pad.

Anca recognized Robyn's farther to the back of the room. She had extra tubes connected to her belly. Her tank was also thicker than the others with extra monitors and keypads. These people did *not* want her taken.

Had they injected her with something? Why had they singled her out? Anca saw Meryem's face brighten: she'd figured out something. She gave the signal for them to continue.

They made their way carefully over the tubes and wires that snaked their way across the floor. It only took them a few minutes, but to Anca it felt like much longer. Her heart was pounding in her chest, the growing buzz of machines a deafening cacophony to her sensitive ears. At last they stood, no longer needing stealth. There weren't even any cameras. Victor was the first to speak. "Irrumabo."

"Fuck is right," said Xerxes. "What the hell is this? How do we get them out? Meryem, did you figure that out?"

"I think so." She walked to the closest panel. Xerxes watched over her shoulder; he was the most tech-savvy of the group. They had a quick discussion about how the control panel connected to the tank and how the tank was constructed. Anca didn't understand most of it. She held formation with the others. *I really need to get back in the game. If I knew more about modern technology, I could help.* She felt completely useless. Her guilt didn't have time to settle in. Xerxes had taken over. He was carefully punching various buttons on the pad, bent close in concentration, his dark curls in his face.

A sucking noise came from the tank. Xerxes had figured out how to drain it. He didn't wait for it to be empty before moving to the next tank. Having watched Xerxes, Meryem went to another tank to drain it as well. If Anca had closed her eyes, she could have convinced herself she was standing on the shore of a white-water river. The rushing sound of water echoed off the walls, making the effect more complete.

At last the first tank was near empty. It was The Ancient that had won the jousting tournament and saved them from being crushed in the explosion. Xerxes was back and punched more buttons. The hissing of air told them he'd been successful. An entire side of the tank swung forward, liquid spilling on the ground. Immediately Chance went forward, pulling out all the tubes. Crumbled on the floor of the tank, The Ancient didn't move.

"Briton, can you hear me?" Chance held her fingers to his throat.

Vampire aging, mathematically, is akin to exponential decay. At first your aging only slows a little. After a century or so, your aging stops completely. This is also true of a vampire's pulse. It never stops completely but, for The Ancients, it can be minutes between heartbeats. They waited. The buzzing of the machines grew louder.

"He's alive!" she declared. Anca exhaled. She'd held her breath without realizing.

"I have Veia. She's alive!" called Meryem from the next tank.

"I have another!" Three Ancients were slid from their watery prisons and brought to the center of the group. Xerxes was frantically at work on another tank when doors slammed open all around. The room was suddenly full of guards, and they weren't all human. The easy fighting was over. The guards spread against the walls encircling them.

In the space of a human heartbeat Anca raised her gun and emptied the weapon. She aimed for their eyes. Even if it didn't kill them, at least they'd be short an eye. She dropped her empty gun with a splash. Before it could hit the ground, she'd already unwrapped the chain around her. Next to her, Xerxes, Meryem and Isobel were all emptying their weapons as well. Anca had the least rounds, so she was out first. Lita was dragging Briton out of the tank, Chance was doing the same with Veia.

When Anca rolled, as she was near the edge of the group, she went slightly sideways. A bullet wouldn't do much to her, but her taking a bullet meant one less hitting their targets. They didn't know yet if these vampires were elders or not, so it was best to assume they were elders, and every bullet would count in taking them down.

Three of the guards had dropped, blood gushing out of an eye creating haunting swirls of red in the clear liquid. Another two guards dropped. Anca popped up from her roll, chain swinging. It thwacked as it sunk into the guard's skull. She let the momentum of the swing wrap the chain around her arm, then let it fly on its next circle, hitting another guard in the shoulder. He dropped his rifle and bared his fangs in challenge. Anca bared her own as she swung again, wrapping the chain around his neck. She pulled on the chain as hard as she could. With a crack, his challenge ended. She rushed forward, chopping of his head with his own knife. She abandoned her chain for his knife and pistol. The fight was becoming tighter, making the chain less effective. She aimed for eyes until she was empty. Then the fighting got nasty.

She slammed a guard into the wall. She felt the knives go through him and hit brick. Another guard came at her during her attack. She kicked out, throwing him off balance slightly. It gave her enough time to remove the knives from her first target and slash the throat of the second guard. Blood sprayed, though if he was an elder he'd heal in a matter of moments.

She returned to her first victim, cutting off his head. She alternated between slashing the chest of the first guard and the second. Bullets sprayed the wall just behind the second guard. One of her friends was covering her, but they wouldn't be able to forever.

After three slices to each guard's chest, Anca plunged both of her hands into the guards' chests. Jerking out their hearts, she dropped them to the ground, picked up her knives and sliced off their heads. She rejoined the fray as the bodies hit the floor with a slap.

Her next target swung his rifle toward her. She caught it mid-swing. Fear showed in the guard's eyes -- his strength was much more than she'd been expecting. No, she was weaker. *How long had it been since I've eaten? Since any of us ate?*

She slammed a flat hand into his chest with enough force to throw him back. Grabbing him by the neck, she slammed him into the wall, crushing his cervical spine. Chance was nearly a blur as she sprinted into the next guard, knee first. Seamlessly, Anca swung for his neck as Chance swung her dirk through his torso. He hit the ground in three pieces.

Anca could hear more guards making their way to the doors. They'd been swarmed in seconds. She looked around. Everyone was showing signs of fatigue and hunger. They wouldn't survive another fight.

"We need to leave!"

Gunfire could be heard outside the next door. Tadashi burst through. Reaching to his left he crushed the neck of the guard that had tried to stop him. He held him up, a shield against the gunfire. Grabbing the guard's rifle, he shot the guards to his right. Leave it to a samurai to be so efficient.

"Everyone, this way!" he called.

When you've fought next to someone for thousands of years the trust is pretty strong. Without question Anca made her way to Tadashi and the others followed. Lita dragging The Ancients. Meryem took Eubule (the third Ancient) from her, draping their mother over her shoulders. With a regretful glance at the remaining Ancients they ran through the door. Bullets hit the door as it shut.

"I thought I would find a way out before getting you," Tadashi explained as they ran down another white hallway.

"Thanks for that," said Meryem. Eubule was bouncing against her back, his tight black curls swaying.

"This way." Tad directed them through a pair of double doors. Two more guards were on the other side. Anca surged forward next to Tad. They decapitated the guards without stopping. The heads hit the floor with a slap and rolled away as the bodies swayed upright for a heartbeat.

Tad turned left down a side hallway. There was a single door on the right near the end. He brought out a hand and an eye from his pocket as they approached. He held the eye up to a retinal scanner and pressed the hand to a palm scanner. After several scans the door opened.

"The others had the right stuff to get out right?" Anca asked Meryem.

"Yes. A hand and a head from two guards in case a door needed two people to open."

"Smart, thank you." Anca thought of Trig. She hoped they had gotten out okay.

"There should be one more door and then we're out," Tad said. They thundered down the hallway, stealth long forgotten.

Anca saw Briton swinging against Lita's back. The Ancients weren't showing any signs of life. Trig had recovered from his sedative in under ten minutes. Whatever they had been given must have been intense.

The door required two retinal scans and... an ear scan. They didn't have an ear.

"Shit!" Meryem began pacing. "I'll be right back." The others parted when she sprinted past.

"Hey!" She was already gone. "I hope the others didn't run into this problem."

"They had heads. They'll be fine," said Tadashi.

A moment later, Meryem was running backwards firing behind her. "Catch!" She tossed a bloody tied off shirt. Inside were two heads. Guards were tight on her tail.

"Get down!" Tad switched the rifle to fully automatic and mowed down the three guards. They pressed the body parts to the scanners. They confirmed the guards' clearance and opened the door.

They ran out into the early morning air.

CHAPTER 12

Now they had a new concern. Where *were* they?

Anca looked around. "Any idea where we are guys?"

"It looks like we're in Greece," said Xerxes.

"How the fuck can you tell that?" asked Maryem. "Never mind." She collected her thoughts as they sprinted away from the lab. They had made it out of the parking lot and were dashing past trees. "Let's find a road sign or something. If we can find out where in Greece we are, I can get us to a bunker."

"Will the others know where to go?" Anca thought of Trig again.

"Hanare will," said Isobel. "He knows where all the bunkers are. He's training for bunker maintenance and surveillance."

Anca nodded, relieved that the others were probably already safe. Her head felt light from the movement.

They came across a backroad. Keeping out of site, they ran along its length for two hours until they came to a sign. "Yes! This way." Meryem had them cross the road then run at an angle opposite of that they had just been running. "We went too far North," she explained.

Anca's heart was pounding in her chest. Each breath cut at her throat. *How long have we been running?*

They sun was beginning to make its way over the horizon. The group had slowed from a sprint to a jogging pace. "The others may already be there," Meryem gasped over her shoulder.

They jogged for another ninety minutes before they came to a cluster of large boulders. Meryem crouched down and lifted up a rock about the size of a head. Beneath there was a key pad with a thumbprint scanner. She entered a seven-digit code and scanned her thumb. A tiny tray the size of a pinky nail popped out. Meryem pressed her finger to her fang until blood welled. She swiped her finger against the tray to fill it with her blood.

The seconds passed, the only sound their gasping breaths and pounding hearts.

A grinding noise came from the smallest boulder in front of them. It started rising. Behind the boulder was a descending case of stairs.

"Okay, let's see if they're here." Meryem replaced the rock.

Anca saw there was metal on the bottom of it and saw the rock replace itself to its original location faster than gravity would have permitted. Electric magnets. That would prevent any human from accidently lifting the rock; they wouldn't have the strength.

Her anticipation grew with each step they descended. *I hope they're okay.* They'd gone down three flights worth when Anca began to hear something. Voices.

They passed through two more doors, a thumb then retinal scan, before arriving to the main room. Relieved cheers erupted all around. Hanare bounded forward lifting Isobel off her feet. She practically wept with relief.

"I knew you'd bring them to safety," she said.

"You look pretty relieved for someone that knew we were okay, baby." Hanare's laugh sounded more like a sob. He held his wife gingerly. She immediately grabbed his arm to inspect how his skin was healing. Slow, slower than it should have been.

"Trig?" Anca scanned the crowd. There were a dozen vampires standing. On the ground there were bodies covered in sheets. Were they all that had been taken? Had they unknowingly left more at the lab? At the time Anca was sure but now… Anca looked back at the sheets. Too many.

"I'm here." Trig made his way forward with Sarah right on his heels. They crushed each other in a hug.

"Hanare led us straight here. Sarah took one look at the stars and knew exactly where we were."

"Stars!" Meryem practically knocked herself out she hit her forehead so hard.

"Anca!"

"Nuru?" Once more Anca was taken into a crushing hug. "I didn't know if you'd been taken…"

"I sent him off with the others. Sorry I didn't tell you," said Meryem.

Anca held Nuru in a tight embrace. She felt herself beginning to break but now was not the time. She pulled away.

"What I want to know is who betrayed us and why were there vampires working with them?" said Anca.

"What?" Trig's head snapped around so fast it nearly broke the sound barrier. "There were vampires? Vampires don't attack other vampires. That's the law," said Trig.

"The first guard I fought was a vampire, as was nearly every guard we fought after we parted ways. There were some at The Gathering. Specially fitted cells, knowledge of The Ancients, knowledge of The Gathering. They had people on the inside." She took a breath. "We have a mole."

"Merde," breathed Nuru.

All vampire bunkers are structured like cozy panic rooms. Completely isolated and constructed to withstand everything from chemical warfare to a nuclear blast. Yet they have forgotten not one creature comfort.

Numerous bedrooms were scattered throughout the bunker. Some were built for comfort, others for capacity. One bedroom contained twelve beds, bunkbed style. Another room had two queen beds with an attached private bathroom. One room had a king-size bed with a jacuzzi bathtub.

Even the kitchen spared no comfort. In addition to the two classic fridges, a giant walk-in fridge contained hundreds of bags of blood. Anytime they came close to expiration a worker would collect them and pass them out to vampires that had just come back from field missions or give them to the chefs to be blended into smoothies. (Waste not want not.)

The kitchen was attached to an expansive dining room. Around one of the tables sat those that had decided discussion was more important that sleep. But not more important than food.

"I don't understand," said Meryem, taking one of the bags of blood that were being passed around. "If they had someone on the inside telling them about us, why were we able to escape?"

"Not all of us," Tad pointed out. "Most of The Ancients are still there."

"Including Robyn." Meryen sat back.

"She was in the back. There was something different about her tank. It was more reinforced than the others. And I could have sworn there were extra tubes going to her stomach," said Anca.

"Well that would make sense," said Meryem, looking thoroughly disturbed. "The big announcement that was never made. Robyn's pregnant. The second trueborn vampire from two ancients in over a thousand years."

"Holy shit." Anca passed a hand over her face. *That's why they took the risk.*

"Yeah, and now they have her." Meryem sipped from her blood bag. "Who were they? Did anyone find out?"

"Church of Heavenly Light," said Anca.

"That's not possible," said Trig. "We ended them."

"They must have risen from the ashes then," said Anca, waving a hand.

"Actually…" Meryem looked at them tentatively.

"Now what?" said Anca and Trig together.

"We've been watching a group for the last seventy years that we thought might be a resurgence of the Church of Cleansing Fire."

What else don't I know?

"Why wasn't this information shared?" Trig's voice was strained as he struggled to stay calm.

"The Ancients forbade it. We never confirmed-"

Anca cut across Meryem. "Did they know about the labs?"

Meryem looked at Anca with a bracing look. "Yes."

"Are fucking kidding me?" Trig was on his feet.

Meryem looked at the table. "We were keeping an eye on them, but we can't watch everything at once, especially trying to keep it quiet."

"You knew?" said Anca.

"Don't lecture me on secrets Anca," said Meryum.

"Never mind, what we need to do is make sure everyone is safe. I for one could use some rest. We already called headquarters?" asked Anca.

"Yes, eighty minutes ago," said Nuru.

"We'll have to call again. That lab we came from wasn't even one we were watching, and they'll want to know about the tracking devices we found in The Ancients," said Meryem. They'd removed the tracking devices but had decided it was best not to destroy them. Destroying them would let whoever was monitoring them know they'd been found. They'd placed them in a bowl of hot water just in case they were rigged to relay a change in temperature.

"We need to go back for the others, but we don't have the strength with just us," said Isobel. "If we'd stayed, we'd be dead right now."

"You mean more dead," said Hanare weakly. They all chuckled, the tension beginning to break.

"There's a reason we left them behind. We simply couldn't get them out to safety," said Isobel. "We should wait. There's still a good deal of a mess at the castle. After they pull away as many as they dare they'll come our way."

"Good, then let's calm our heads and decide our next move when they get here. I don't think any of us are in the right state to make decisions," said Anca.

Meryem looked away from Anca's gaze. Her withholding information, even under orders from The Ancients, had cost lives.

Anca pushed her chair back and rose. The others dispersed about the bunker. She had no intention of going to bed. Her arms were sticky with blood. Plunging them into a basin sink she began scrubbing, trying not to think about Derya.

A bottle tapped her right shoulder. Looking behind her, she saw Nuru holding a whiskey labeled Montana 1884. "You know me too well." She grabbed the bottle and drank from it straight. A nostalgic calm crept its way down her throat, flooding into her limbs.

"Figured you could use a drink after that hell hole." His white clothes were covered in dirt. A spray of blood at his collar looked like he'd had a bloody nose at one point. He handed her the bottle.

"That's the thing that worries me. It wasn't that much of a hell hole. I ripped off my restraints with some help from Urian. So did some of the others. We got pinched at the end but if they were able to capture us why were we able to get away?" She handed him back the bottle. He took a swig. "Why were we able to get out Nuru? I keep feeling like we were *supposed* to escape. It only became impossible when we started breaking out The Ancients."

"That's unsettling." He took a long pull from the bottle. "You think The Ancients were the real targets?"

"They were all there. All of The Ancients had never been in one place before this. But no, I don't think they were the main target, just a bonus. I think the main target was Robyn."

"Specifically, her unborn child," he said, handing back the bottle. Anca nodded, taking it. "I repeat, unsettling. What do those people want with an unborn vampire child?" muttered Nuru.

"My doctor said something about splicing the virus." Her face slackened as she remembered something else. "He also said if you want a good test result, you need pure ingredients. You can't get a purer form of the vampire virus than the child of two Ancients. But why not kidnap a vampire child that's already born?"

"An infant is less of a threat and we haven't had a child like this in over a thousand years. Plus, there's the possibility they can train it, convert it to their cause. That child will be strong, a better ally than enemy."

Anca rubbed her temples, trying to process it all. Nuru looked at her with concern. "Can we go somewhere private to talk?"

She led him to one of the rooms. Most of the bunkbeds were full so she led him to a room that had two queen beds inside. Nuru sputtered the words in a rush. "I just wanted to express my apologies --"

"Don't bother. You did what you could." Anca sat heavily on the bed. "We shouldn't have left them there."

Nuru walked to the bed. "I meant Derya."

Anca bit her lip. "She'd just turned. She hadn't even really started her studies at the conservatory." She closed her eyes, willing the tears to hold back. "She thought she was saving me. I could have taken a machete and lived."

"But she got shot too. Anca, it wasn't your fault."

She leaned into him letting him support her for the first time in years. Thinking of Derya was too much. "I'm sorry I didn't believe you before. I'm a soldier. You were right. The moment the attack happened I was nothing else." Anca looked at Nuru. "You held your own pretty well."

"Just trying to keep up." He brushed a strand of her hair out of her face. "I don't want you to deny who you are. No one can be happy if they lie about what they are. Especially if that lie is to themselves."

"You know sometimes your philosophical background is very pronounced."

Nuru chuckled. "I suppose you find that irritating."

"I find it endearing." She looked into his eyes. A million thoughts flew across her mind.

"You do, don't you?" he asked.

Nodding, Anca leaned in, she intended to finish what they'd started a day ago, before this chaos had started.

She half expected him to pull away. He leaned in. When their lips touched she wondered why she'd ever doubted his passion. He didn't just meet her kiss, he pulled her in.

Anca met him with equal enthusiasm. "I'm sorry," he breathed when they pulled apart. "I should have done that long ago."

"I guess you'll just have to make up for lost time." She pulled him toward her. They let the stresses of the day slough away in each other's embrace.

CHAPTER 13

A loud knocking on the door woke Anca.

"What?"

"The Ancients are waking up."

Anca immediately jumped into some clothes. She opened the door wearing unbuttoned pants and an oversized shirt she'd found in a drawer. "Where are they?"

Anca and Nuru walked to the center of the main room where the Ancients had been put on cots. The other vampires hadn't wanted them out of their sight. Isobel had been giving them every second of her attention that wasn't given to Hanare. She was chatting and checking Briton's pulse. "He's hurt but he'll be okay."

"His smile is brighter than the sun and steadier than the pull of gravity," said Briton to Isobel. "I'm sorry this happened."

"Who else was hurt? Did we lose anyone?" Veia seemed almost in a panic.

Anca spoke. "We lost Janelle --"

"Hada?"

"She locked herself in that room a few hours ago," said Lita.

Anca felt sick. Hada had seemed like she was handling everything well. She should have known it was temporary. How many times had she held herself together for the sake of those around her only to break down completely when she was alone?

Veia, swaying, got to her feet. Anca rushed to help her but she raised a hand in protest. Veia took a deep breath and, without a word, went slowly to the room Hada had locked herself in.

"A single casualty?" asked Eubule disbelieving. He was struggling to achieve a sitting position.

"No," said Trig.

"Where's my wife? Where's Robyn?" asked Eubule. He looked around as if she was just behind one of the onlookers, his dark eyes hungry for the sight of her.

"We couldn't get the rest of The Ancients. She's still their captive," confessed Meryem.

Eubule lost what progress he had made in his attempt to sit. He slumped against the pillows. Anca scolded herself. She had been so busy trying to kill as many people as possible she hadn't seen who else they'd lost. Janelle and Derya had been enough to process. Now that she thought about it there were many she couldn't account for.

"Who else did we lose?" Briton asked.

"Derya," Anca choked out.

"Willow, Wayne, Daniel, Ian…" Goran kept listing off names. Tears began to spill down his face. Anca felt numb. So many, they'd lost so many. Eubule and Briton's faces turned stony as Goran kept listing names.

Veia came out of the room with her arm around Hada. Veia looked up at them all then at Briton and Eubule. "We have sins to confess and a family to protect," she said.

Briton and Eubule looked at each other and nodded. "Where can we hold a meeting?" asked Eubule.

Trig waved a hand at the large dining table. "How about right here?"

"We'll need some privacy-" said Briton slowly.

"I don't think you do," growled Trig.

"He's right. The time for secrets is past," said Veia firmly.

Eubule nodded. "Secrets cost us lives today. They very well may have cost me my wife and child." He saw the lack of surprise on everyone's faces. "That Robyn is with child is already known to you."

"I told them," said Meryem.

"She was being held in a special tank. I thought it was odd. Meryem explained why she had been kept differently than the rest," said Anca.

"We were in tanks?" Veia looked surprised as she pulled out a chair for Hada.

"Meryem and Xerxes figured out how to get them open. We must have been watched because you were barely out before we were surrounded." Anca gestured to Eubule and sat down.

"We were outmatched. They must have sent those reinforcements the moment we entered that place you were being kept. There were only a few guards before then, most of them human. But when we got to you there were more guards than we could handle and almost all of them were vampires." Meryem pleaded with her eyes. "We had to leave. We would have all been killed."

"You did what you could," said Briton. "We were helpless. Even if you had stayed to get the rest out of the tanks, they'd still be captives. You had to carry us out I believe?" Everyone nodded. "Then there was no possible better outcome. By saving us and yourselves, you saved as many as you could. We would all be dead if you'd stayed longer."

"Robyn would have wanted you all safe," said Eubule begrudgingly.

"Yes, she would," said Veia. She sat at the head of the table and rolled her shoulders. She straitened her back and addressed everyone. "We have sinned. We have lied. We Ancients thought ourselves to be protecting those younger than us. We were foolish. With age comes pride, a false sense of earned superiority. Simply because you have survived the passing of time does not mean you have earned respect or knowledge." She licked her lips and looked down at the table. "We lied." She met their gaze once more. "We suspected there was a threat and told no one."

Eubule spoke. "We suspected. We suspected, we did not *know*."

"We knew enough," said Veia. "I have failed my children."

Trig spoke, "The security should have held."

"The security was sound I checked it myself," said Briton. "Mother is right. The fault of this lies squarely on our shoulders."

Anca spoke, "The fault lies with those that attacked us. We didn't attack ourselves. Someone decided to take our Ancients and kill our young. No vampire here is cruel enough to ever do such a thing." She looked at Trig. He didn't meet her gaze.

"Spoken wisely," said Veia.

"Someone has my wife and the rest of The Ancients," said Eubule. "We need to find them. I will not abandon my child, and we do not abandon our own."

"True," said Briton, "but who has them? Why did they attack us? These are the questions that will lead us to them."

Veia put her hands together on the table. "What do we know?"

Just then there was the sound of thundering feet down the front stairwell. A woman with pixie-cut chestnut hair led a group of soldiers down the stairway and into the main room. She was carrying her helmet with her rifle loose at her side. All of them were wearing battle gear with their faces flushed as if they'd just come back from a fight.

"Mother!" The woman said in surprise. She bowed her head, so did the rest of the soldiers.

"Tria, what news?"

"We just came from the lab where you all were kept. There's nothing there."

"The Ancients?" Eubule stood, his eyes pleading.

"Gone," said Tria.

"What *did* you find?" asked Meryem.

"Empty tanks, blown up computers, most of the place was in flames. Some walls even showed signs of acid damage. These people know how to cover their tracks."

A man stepped forward, taking off his helmet. "There's a team sweeping for clues now. We were supposed to just be an extraction team, but unfortunately our services weren't needed." He had a well-trimmed mustache and small beard that he scratched thoroughly after having freed his face from the constriction of the helmet. "If there's anything to find they'll find it."

Eubule sat heavily in his chair looking unconvinced. Briton put a hand on his shoulder.

"They will find something," said Briton.

Eubule nodded.

Meryem stepped forward. "What can we do?"

"Stay safe," said Veia. "We need to get somewhere safe. We are far too close to that place for me to find comfort."

"Step ahead 'a you," said Tria. "There are cars waiting outside to take us all to an airstrip where you'll board a plane and head to the castle of your choice. They await your decision."

"You knew we were awake?" asked Veia.

"We hoped," said Tria heavily.

Veia nodded. "We will discuss it." The Ancients huddled together and spoke rapidly to one another. Several moments later Briton addressed them all.

"New Zealand. It is our newest castle and not that far. This enemy may be old, but they are advanced. We need every edge we can get. Our castle in New Zealand is our safest bet." He nodded to Tria.

She nodded. "To Castle Hukarere Hou."

CHAPTER 14

The sound of jet engines grew louder as Anca clipped her safety belt. "Your choosing New Zealand had nothing to do with visiting your daughter I'm sure," she said to Briton.

"The healers there are excellent." He looked at Hanare. Briton was quite fond of Hanare, that his face had not yet healed hadn't escaped Briton's notice.

"Isobel will take good care of him."

"Of that I have no doubt." Briton gave her a stiff smile.

Anca looked toward the back of the plane where Derya's body was covered with a white sheet. There were small splotches of red over her heart and the side of her head. Anca tore her eyes away before they revealed the depth of her sorrow.

"I believe we were told there were secrets to spill," said a vampire across from Anca.

Veia looked over at them. Briton spoke. "We knew there might be a threat. We increased security for The Gathering. We thought that would be enough."

"That's why you asked Nuru and I for that last-minute consultation," Trig explained, more to himself than anyone else.

Nuru nodded next to Anca. "We put extra layers of magickal protection as well."

"I remember," said Anca. She recalled the second sigil on the ground.

"It was necessary," Nuru said. "But not enough. They must have someone spying on us."

"Or someone's," said Anca. "But we are getting off the point. "Veia, you said you had sins to confess."

There was stilling. Everyone on the plane ceased conversations and looked up. Veia stood to address the attentive faces.

"For seventy years we have suspected that an old enemy has reemerged. The Church of Cleansing Fire --"

"Why wasn't this information shared?" Trig was trying to stay calm.

"We didn't think it was something that everyone needed to know," said Briton.

"We were tortured!" Trig sprang to his feet. "Vampires are dead!"

Veia turned fierce. "You think for a single instant that if I had genuine fear that even one vampire would get hurt, I wouldn't have acted? You forget your place Trygve, remember it."

Trig sat down slowly.

"We Ancients have endured pain you have not known, nor will you while I am still alive." Veia looked at them all. "We will be meeting with those who have investigated this over the years. Fan is one of our best operatives. She will brief us all when we arrive. Until then I will tell you this: I am sorry. We should have shared what information we had sooner. This attack --"

Hanare gave a great heaving cough, spilling blood onto the floor.

"Hanare?!" Isobel clutched at him, frantic to understand what was happening. He coughed again spilling more blood onto the carpet.

Veia looked at Meryem, Anca, anyone who had been in the labs. "What was he exposed to?"

Hada heaved blood onto the floor.

Lita jumped to her side. "Oh God," she gasped.

"What's wrong with us?" Hanare said between spits.

"I'll find out. I'll get you better," promised Isobel.

Others began coughing up blood. Anca looked around in panic. "How long before we land?"

The plane landed in chaos. Over a dozen vampires were coughing up blood with more starting every few minutes. Isobel took command, sickness was her specialty. "Follow me. As fast as you can. This way."

Wheelchairs and stretchers were waiting for them when they landed. Hanare was strapped down to a stretcher, he had started having convulsions.

Isobel looked frantic yet somehow still in control. "Those who aren't sick help those who are. This way!"

Anca and Nuru each took an arm of an ailing vampire and lifted them off the ground, sprinting after Isobel. The sick bay was massive with white walls. The floor was covered in large patches of dirt as if it had been spilled in a hurry.

"Asia by the North wall. African soils by the West wall." A man with perfectly styled short dreads, dark skin, and startling green eyes was yelling out directions. Anca sometimes forgot Veia had a son. He was older than Anca by a couple thousand years. Anca only saw him every couple centuries. He and his mother saw each other every few decades but when you're both over five thousand years old, frequent visits aren't necessary. Especially when you both have time-intensive jobs. Fatin was the head of Castle Hukarere Hou.

Moon priestesses and priests were running among the doctors to help where they could. Many vampires shied away from them. Some of the Moon priests and priestesses were werewolves. The species were friendly, but many vampires were still wary of the werewolves.

A vampire sprinted up to Fatin with a young-looking woman draped over his shoulder. He shoved past a werewolf priestess. "What of soil from the Yukon?"

Fatin's eyes bulged in panic. "We don't have any." His rich voice dripped with regret. He turned to a helper next to him. "Order some, now!" She nodded curtly, her phone seemed to materialize in her hand and she started speaking rapid French.

"You don't have any? You'll house these creatures but won't supply the necessities for your own people? What if she doesn't heal quick enough without it?"

"We'll do what we can." Fatin placed a reassuring hand on the man's shoulder. He shrugged it off. "Come." He directed him toward a circle of unaffected witches. They placed the woman with two other vampires within the circle the witches had formed. They hoped their magick would tie over those whose birthing soil wasn't there until they could be provided better help. Nuru saw the circle and looked at Anca. She gave him a nod, taking the sick vampire they'd been carrying completely. He ran to lend his magick to the circle.

Anca walked toward Veia and Fatin who were talking rapidly after dropping off her sick vampire onto some soil from Venezuela. "Any ideas on what this is?"

"We're getting tests ready," said Fatin. "Everyone will get swabbed, blood samples taken... everything."

"We're doing all we can," said Veia.

The werewolves weren't welcomed by the desperate. They sat in a corner to keep their smell away from those that did not want them there. They offered their prayers to the sick regardless.

"I've heard that before," said Anca, perhaps a bit more bitterly than she should have.

A helper ran up to Veia and whispered in her ear so quietly Anca couldn't hear a word. Veia eyes grew wide.

"What is it?" asked Anca.

Veia gestured for Anca and Fatin to follow her. When they reached a secluded hallway, she turned.

"This disease, whatever it is, isn't just here. We just got world from two other castles in Japan and Uruguay. They are experiencing the same sickness. All the vampires affected are less than two hundred years old, but not every vampire under two hundred years old is affected." Veia gave her son an apprehensive look.

"Over half of our population in under two hundred," said Fatin.

"I know," said Veia. She had a silent moment of understanding with her son.

"We've been infiltrated," he said, nodding slowly.

"Some of the attackers at The Gathering were vampires. Most of the guards that attacked us when we rescued you were too," said Anca, pointing at Veia with her chin. Veia and Fatin seemed to be slowly pushing Anca out of the conversation with their words. She wanted to remind them that she was one of the reasons Veia was even still alive.

Fatin shook his head, his short dreads swaying. "This can't just be the church. They hate vampires; they'd never side with them. What if it's --"

"I know," said Veia, she looked pained. "It seems the only logical option."

"What?" Anca's nerves were near their end. "Who is doing this?"

"Family," Veia muttered.

Fatin put a hand on his mother's shoulder. "Whoever is doing this is attacking family."

"That's not what she --"

Isobel came around the corner flanked by two other vampires dressed like doctors. "We need samples from you too, now."

"Things are starting to turn for the worse," said the man to Isobel's left.

"Isobel go be with your husband," said Veia. She went to her and guided her back toward the main room.

"This conversation isn't over," said Anca. Veia gave her a heavy look.

"Remember your place Anca," said Fatin.

"And you remember what's at stake here. Our species could die because of your secrets." She turned on her heel and stormed off.

CHAPTER 15

Twenty more vampires died that day. Isobel clutched at her husband as he shook so hard he almost flung himself out of his pod. He had a single moment of clarity near the end. "Don't stop smiling," he told his wife. Convulsions overtook him after that that were so hard they broke his spine in two places. He spewed out more blood and then stopped moving. It was a horrifying end for someone who had brought so much joy to their lives. Isobel's screams were still echoing in Anca's head hours later.

Anca hadn't been able to process the pain at first. Hanare was like the sun, always there waiting to bring light and warmth to your life. His death was as incomprehensible as someone saying the sun had flickered out.

Soil for every vampire was eventually delivered. For some it had come too late. The woman from the

Yukon had died an hour before her soil arrived. The man that carried her blamed Fatin. He said she would have lived if the soil had been there, had she not had the added stress of werewolves nearby, that Fatin was incompetent and uncaring about his charges. Veia had suggested he go for a long swim to cool off. Last Anca heard, he was still swimming in the Pacific.

She went to find Lita; she needed her anchor. She found her in the nursery. Lita loved children: it's why she had become a family lawyer in recent years. Vampire children were a rarity. The nursery was empty.

"Hey," said Anca.

"Hey," said Lita.

"What are you doing staring at empty cribs?"

"Hoping they'll fill."

"It would be nice to have more children around," said Anca.

They were silent a long moment. "I want kids," said Lita.

"A woman needs to have sex with a man to get pregnant last I checked."

They have methods now where you don't actually need to have sex to get pregnant."

"I'd nearly forgotten."

"Do you think it could work for vampires?"

"It'd be worth a shot," said Anca. "Pregnancy can be dangerous, even for vampires, but you would make a great mother. I would love to meet a mini you."

They looked at each other a moment. "Assuming we live that long."

"Would you think me shallow if I started sleeping around just to get pregnant?" She looked at Anca.

Anca was a little thrown. "That sounds like a bit of a moral dilemma," Anca looked at the empty cribs. "I suppose if you slept around with no consideration for their feelings about the whole thing, I might have a problem with it. But if you told these guys what you were trying to do… I think you'd find a lot of willing and understanding guys." She looked back at Lita.

Lita looked at her with mild surprise. "So basically, if I tell these guys I'm just using them for their sperm, you'd be cool with it?"

Anca shrugged and nodded. "I'm not the one trying to get knocked up. This is up to you and whoever is willing to part with their sperm."

Lita smiled. "I've wanted to be a mother since I was a child."

"I know."

"I never thought, even after I turned, that it could be a possibility."

"Being a vampire can heal all sorts of things, but we ovulate weird. This could take a long time," said Anca.

"I'm going to find Urian." Lita began walking away.

"Urian?"

Lita turned. "To see if he'd jizz in a cup for the sake of the species." Lita gave her a playful smile and left. Anca grinned. *That baby will be flirting before it walks.* Her grin faded. Flirting had made her think of Nuru. *I should find him.*

On her way to find Nuru, she found Trig. "Is Sarah okay? I haven't seen her."

"She isn't sick." He waved behind Anca, she turned to see Sarah put down a bio-waste bag and start walking over. Anca let out a breath.

"Have you seen Nuru? I need to apologize," said Anca.

"More apologizing? You didn't do enough at the bunker?"

"Not that kind." She punched him in the arm. She looked at him seriously. "Are you okay?"

"I am," he said. Sarah stood at his side and put her hand in his.

"I'll take care of him. I always do," said Sarah. Anca nodded. Sarah had been a great girlfriend to Trig over the years. Anca still didn't understand their relationship, how they could spend so much time apart but be so in love. Yet when it really mattered, when things were at their worst, there was Sarah, her devotion unwavering.

"Those that were sick and survived have stopped getting worse. They still vomit blood from time to time, but no one new has gotten sick in a while, so we think the disease is slowing down. The witches were told to rest up, as they've been at it for hours. I think you'll find them down there." Sarah pointed toward a hallway leading away from the main room.

"Thanks." She gave them both a brief hug.

Anca walked down the hall with apprehension. She needed to apologize, but how do you summarize a century of regret? And was it regret? She thought about her decision to walk away from fighting and concentrate on the conservatory. No, that she didn't regret it. The gryphons were too adorable for her to regret spending so much time with them. Just being around them had quieted the death screams that sometimes creeped into her head.

But she had distanced herself from Nuru before that. He'd wanted to know her completely and she'd shut him out. There were things in her past she didn't share with anyone. Even Lita didn't know everything.

Anca gave a heavy exhale. Nuru had been right all along. She was a soldier. The moment her family had been threatened she'd jumped into the fight. She hated it when Nuru was right about something like this. It had been part of why they'd broken up: she hated being the one with an inferior mind. She could beat him in hand to hand combat any day, but when it came to logic and strategy, it wasn't even close: his mind was far superior. She rolled her shoulders. Nuru had always said part of what makes a strong mind is admitting weakness, acknowledging wrongs. Well he'd been right about her not being able to stop being a soldier so maybe she should give this a try too.

She found him in one of the lounge rooms overlooking the mountains. An entire wall was glass interrupted only by a stone fireplace that stretched from the wall to cut the massive room in two. On one side there were overstuffed couches and chairs. On the other side were round tables and wooden chairs. A group with tired eyes were sitting around one of the tables playing a noncommitmental game of poker. Nuru was sitting on one of the sofas, a leg stretched out. He seemed to be gazing out the massive window without actually seeing the swirling snow.

"May I sit?"

Nuru took her by the arm and pulled her into his lap. "How are things down there?" he asked.

"Sarah said things have stopped getting worse."

"I'm glad she's okay. She is young enough we thought she would get sick." His tone suggested a question.

"She's fine. I just talked to her. She wasn't showing any symptoms." Nuru nodded against her shoulder. "How are you? Doing magick that long must have left you exhausted."

"I will be alright after I rest. I know magick can't cure it but --"

"But everything helps."

Nuru took a breath. "I've had a lot of time to think while we were apart. I know I'm not going to know everything about you, and I'm okay with that now. Our time in the bunker was really special to me."

"I'm sorry," said Anca.

"For the bunker? You weren't that bad."

"What --?" She turned to face him. "Not what I meant. I know I'm a pleasure when I pleasure. Fuck you."

"Again? If you insist."

She shook her head laughing. "I'm sorry…" She warned him not to interrupt with her eyes. "For not listening to you."

He tilted his head. "Not listening to what?"

"That I can't… not be a soldier."

"You're a fighter Anca. One of the fiercest I've ever met. Lying to yourself about who you are only causes pain. A witch who doesn't practice," he gestured to himself, "blinds themselves to the power pulsing all around them and struggle to understand why they feel so alone." He gestured to her. "A fighter who doesn't fight, feels guilt over those they could have saved. Retiring was never your path just as turning a blind eye to the energies around me was never an option for me."

"Your teacher would be proud."

"What he would be we will never know. I'm glad you've accepted who you are."

She nuzzled into his arms and allowed herself to drink in the pleasure of being against him. "I'm sorry I wasted so much time."

"You needed to learn who you are for yourself. That is a journey worth taking no matter how long it takes."

Anca woke up in Nuru's arms on the couch overlooking the mountains. They were so different than the ones of her home. Where Romanian mountains were rich and green, these mountains were white and harsh. She turned her head to watch the flames dance in the fireplace.

What else don't I know?

Why had Marcial been aksed to challenge Veia's rule? What was going to happen with that? Did someone break into the library when their security was down? How had the vampires been infected? What were they sick with? Who had attacked them? How many had died? Could they cure those still sick? Would Lita manage to get knocked up?

Anca sat up slowly so as not to wake up Nuru. He stirred slightly but remained asleep. *He must have really spent himself.* Anca looked into his face, how the firelight danced against his dark skin. How could she have wasted so many years? It was such a simple thing he'd wanted from her: admit who you are.

She stepped slowly to the wall of glass to peer at the mountains beyond. Where the mountains of Romania made her feel small and sad, these mountains made her feel powerful and hopeful. They needed that hope. Over half of their population was at risk of being infected with whatever disease their attackers had set on them. When had they been infected? It couldn't have been the labs, the disease was too far spread, vampires that hadn't made any contact with those had been taken to the labs were sick. Anca thought back. If they weren't infected in the labs they must have been infected at some other time. When would have been the best time to infect as many vampires as possible? She closed her eyes in concentration.

When?

Her eyes snapped open and she sprinted toward the sick bay.

"Where's Isobel? I need to talk to a healer," Anca demanded.

"I'm a healer." An older looking man with substantial eyebrows stepped forward.

"I think I know when they were infected."

His eyes grew bigger. "Come with me." He waved her forward. He brought her to a large office with a tiny window with a view of the mountains off the sick bay. He pressed a couple buttons on the phone on his desk and then gestured toward a chair for her to sit in. She ignored it.

"The Gathering. The canisters," she said.

He understood at once. "That's why they made the risk. They were able to infect most of our population in one swing. But why wait until some had already drunk? We were just breaking the fast when they attacked."

"I think they were delayed by the last-minute additions to our security measures. That may be why we were able to escape too. They had set up those restraints assuming they would be dealing with starved vampires," said Anca.

The office door opened. Briton, Eubule, Veia, Fatin, and Isobel entered. "What's going on?" asked Fatin.

The healer spoke. "Anca may have just solved some of our mysteries."

"Please explain Anca," said Veia.

"I think those extra security measures Trig and Nuru approved are the only reason any of us were able to get out of those labs. I think they delayed the attack at The Gathering just long enough for us to drink and get the strength that allowed us to escape. I think those that attacked us designed the labs with the assumption that we'd all be starved. I also think the canisters that they knocked us out with also had whatever disease that's been killing the young in them."

Briton spoke, "If they had planned on killing us all at The Gathering, why take us to the labs?"

"I don't know. Maybe they brought us to cause more panic. That way, those that were left behind would be more likely to flee. Spread the disease quicker," said Anca.

Fatin nodded.

"The labs were labeled," said Isobel. "They knew who they were going to grab. It wasn't a last-minute decision."

"Which brings us back to why did they kidnap us?" said Anca.

Eubule was nodding, "This is good progress."

"We barely learned anything," muttered Anca.

"We learned that whoever attacked us didn't know of the last-minute additions to our security. We learned that whoever attacked us had the ultimate goal of kidnapping The Ancients and, in all probability, my wife and child. We learned that whoever attacked us wants the rest of you dead." Eubule stared with unfocused eyes. "We have a long list of enemies, but this has narrowed it down greatly."

Fatin took out his phone and dialed. Anca heard ringing and a young voice answer. "What did we do with the canisters from Castle Acasă? Good, I want to know everything there is to know about those canisters." He hung up and looked at them all. "If there's anything to learn from those cannisters, we'll know within a couple days."

"We already took blood samples from everyone too," said Isobel. "That should give us a better idea about what's killing everyone."

"Any progress on that?" asked Anca.

Isobel shook her head. "All we know is that it was in everyone's blood."

"Everyone's?" Anca suddenly felt like her veins were itchy.

Isobel nodded. "Everyone was infected, but not everyone got sick. Whatever this is isn't strong enough to hurt the older vampires."

There was a tense silence. "So, what do we do in the meantime?" asked Anca.

"Help the sick, comfort those that have lost loved ones, and prepare ourselves," said Briton.

"Prepare ourselves for what?" said Anca.

"To fight back," he said simply.

CHAPTER 16

Anca and Nuru spent the rest of the day mopping up puke blood and fetching supplies for the healers. It was tiring work. Not because of the physical exertion, Anca could run for an entire day before she started to feel tired, it was the emotional tole that was high. The sickness had slowed down but those most affected were still at risk. At any moment Anca could turn around and see a vampire taking their last raged breath.

Nuru was handling things better. He put hands on every sick vampire he came to. Around dinner time, Anca pulled him aside.

"You need to slow down. You'll exhaust yourself, and then you won't be help to anyone. Come on, let's get something to eat."

He gave her a weary half grin and let her guide him toward the feeding area.

"What's your pleasure?" she asked, gesturing toward a fridge filled with smoothies. The labels read Raspberry Fruitarian or Chocolate Carnivore.

"You," he winked. "I'll take the chocolate."

Anca grabbed the bottle and another labeled Spinach Mixed.

"That is very healthy of you."

"Briton's right. We need to prepare ourselves." She took a healthy swig and led him toward a sitting area.

"We need to learn," Nuru said wisely.

Anca raised her eyebrows.

"We need to learn what this sickness is. More importantly we need to know where they are keeping the antidote."

Anca tilted her head with narrowed eyes.

"They have to have an antidote. They wouldn't have unleashed something like that without knowing they were safe from it."

"Have you discussed this with The Ancients?"

"I mentioned it to them. The witches have been meditating for a way to see a solution, some since the attack at The Gathering."

"I hope it works," said Anca.

Both of their phones rang. "A council meeting? Now?" Anca looked at Nuru. "I guess we should clean up and check it out."

They descended a set of curving gray stairs to a windowless room. Veia and Fatin were deep in a whispered conversation. Anca clenched her fist when she saw some of the other guests, Kali and Marcial were there. Nuru took her hand gently but firmly, a reminder to keep her temper in check.

Trig and Sarah were there as well. Many younger vampires were present. Odd for a council meeting. Kali looked up briefly then returned to flipping through the papers before her. Marcial glanced up and then whispered in Kali's ear, she nodded.

Lita and Urian were also sitting at the large black table. Lita had foregone her usual cleavage-showing attire for an outfit that looked oddly professional. Anca raised an eyebrow at her. Lita had an uncomfortable look on her face.

"What's wrong?" Anca whispered.

"They don't have the equipment for artificial invitro here," said Lita.

"…and?"

"We decided to try the old-fashioned way," Urian said with a strain.

"Oh," said Anca.

Urian opened and closed his mouth a few times. "It felt oddly wrong."

Lita nodded. Anca sat next to her. "Well, you two are very close I'm sure it is going to be awkward at first."

Nuru sat next to her. "Why does Urian look like that?" he asked.

"I'll explain later." Anca put a hand on his knee.

A few more vampires descended the stairs and took their seats. Among them was Briton's daughter. She sat next to her father, tucking a lock of her short blond hair behind her ear. Large monitors flicked to life showing five other rooms similar to the one that they sat in across the globe. Anca recognized one as the werewolf council. This council meeting wasn't just happing in New Zealand: every major castle around the globe was participating. Whatever was about to be discussed must be important.

Veia rose, "A meeting has been called." She glanced at Kali who had a smug look on her face. "All ages are here as all ages have been and will be affected by what we discuss. The fate of our family will be decided. Our entire family must participate." She waved as the screens. Those gathered around the tables shown on the screens nodded solemnly.

Anca tightened her grip on Nuru's knee. He covered her hand with his own.

Veia continued, "I promised to confess our sins." She looked at Anca, she looked back. Her gaze was steady but not harsh. Veia looked down at the table.

The room was filled with murmurs. Veia raised a hand for silence, she was given it. "This family is not the only family of vampires." Whispers budded in every council. Anca clenched her jaw.

Kali cut in. "You were aware of this threat and yet did nothing! Your incompetence, the both of you," she pointed from Fatin to Veia, "has resulted in the spilling of vampire blood."

"Know your place, Kali," said Briton. His daughter's eyes hardened next to him.

"How am I to know my place in the presence of such secrets? I had thought you unfit to rule before. Now I know it," Kali spat.

"And how convenient that such claims were put forth mere days before the attack," said Anca coolly.

"Speak plainly," said Briton.

"Does no one else think it odd that Marcial is requested by someone to ask our Mother to step down, and days later we are attacked? And now she speaks of incompetence when it is because of our Mother and her insistence for increased security at the last minute that any of us are alive." Anca stared at Kali.

"Enough, Anca," said Veia.

Anca sat: she hadn't realized she'd risen to her feet.

"The timing is questionable, but the claims hold truth," said Veia.

The werewolf council representative spoke, "Why were we not informed of this?"

"It was not deemed prudent," said Veia. Veia directed a strange look to the werewolves.

"We put our lives on the line for your preservation, and you think that an ancient enemy like this is not prudent?"

"You put your lives on the line for your own preservation as much as ours," said Fatin. Veia placed a gentle hand on his shoulder. He sat back in his chair.

"Were these the sins you meant to confess," Nuru's deep voice drew everyone's attention, "or is there more?"

Veia exchanged a heavy look with Briton and Eubule. "There is more."

"Of course, there is." Muttered a vampire sitting across from Anca.

They focused their attention on Veia. "We have suspected for nearly a century that the threat of the Church of Cleansing Fire may have resurfaced. Fan, if you will?"

A French woman wearing red lipstick took Veia's place.

"Thank you mother and fellow attendees."

Nuru gripped Anca's hand and shook it slightly. She'd been rolling her eyes. She couldn't help it. This was a council meeting, not a graduation speech.

Fan told them that for the past seventy years they'd been following a group they thought could be a resurgence of the Church of Cleansing Fire, the one they thought they'd extinguished centuries ago. The name hadn't been a big enough flag as there were thousands of churches with similar names. A name alone wasn't enough to damn a group. She revealed that she'd joined the church giving regular confessions, attending baptisms, she even frequented the quilt making. It had seemed like a regular church to her. She'd had to be careful. Over the years it became harder for her to avoid being photographed needing to leave events early and, eventually, the church entirely. Others rotated in, but Fan still headed the investigation. Nothing overly suspicious was ever found other than documents that were from the

Church of Cleansing Fire. It looked more like they were holding the records than actually had a connection with the church.

As much as Anca hated to admit it, she was starting to see why they weren't told about any of this before: there really wasn't anything to tell. There was a church that had records from the Church of Cleansing Fire and had a similar name. Hardly an imminent threat.

"To bring us back to present…" Fan adjusted her papers. "Our forensics team was able to extract some important clues from the lab." She passed around a few pictures, a microchip on a melted desk next to a pair of glasses, a charred yellow file in a metal drawer, glass vials, smashed and whole syringes, and what looked like water-damaged employment files.

"What are we to make of this?" asked Kali.

"Let me explain." Fan held up the picture of the syringes. "These were collected by Lita. Samples have already been sent to our labs for analysis. Hopefully we'll learn more about why we were brought to that lab."

Lita gave a tense nod.

Fan picked up the picture of the charred yellow file. "This was a list of some of the abducted. Next to the names was their status, Ancient, nonancient, magick, or nonmagick user. As far as we can tell they didn't know that elders were their own category."

"They aren't. That hasn't been voted in yet." Kali said as if she was explaining that blue and yellow made green to a five-year-old. She looked down her nose at Fan.

"The reason we will be voting on it is because there is a difference. On the list there was also punishments," continued Fan.

"Punishments?" Trig leaned forward.

Fan looked at him. "For crimes against the species. My guess is you were taken because of your work on synthetic blood."

Trig's jaw clenched. He tightened his clasped hands until his knuckles turned white. Sarah bumped her shoulder against his. He gave her a grateful sideways glance and put his hands in his lap. She put her head on his shoulder.

Whoever had abducted them had a very old way of thinking. Why else would they have dealt out such a severe punishment just for research? Anca listened more intently. Anything she could learn about their attackers brought her closer to punishing those that had orchestrated Trig's rape. She took her hand off Nuru's knee and leaned forward, fully engaged.

Fan held up the picture of the microchip, "This was one of the most important finds. You'll notice all our healers are missing. On this chip was information about the virus. We found out it peaks twice. Once roughly forty-eight hours after infection and again two weeks after infection. The second peak is what has us concerned and why until further notice anyone that hasn't been exposed to the virus is in quarantine."

"How bad will the second peak be?" asked Nuru.

"Basically, if you aren't an Ancient there's a good chance you'll die," said Fan.

All around the table and on the screens, mouths opened in surprise.

The werewolf council looked frightened and confused. "Why are we being told this? Do you think this has something to do with our werewolves disappearing in the America's? Is this disease transferable to werewolves?"

"It doesn't look like either," said Fan. "But we're still looking into it."

"You are being told because we've kept you out of the loop long enough," said Veia.

Nuru picked up the photograph. "How did this survive? That's acid damage on the desk."

"A stroke of luck," said Fan. "The chip was under a pair of glasses. The glass protected the chip."

"Witches have been meditating for a way to see the threat. I guess the powers that be have a sense of humor." Nuru put down the picture with a humorless grin.

"All that I've told you came from invaluable finds, but this," she put forward the picture of the employment files, "was by far the most helpful."

"Employment records? How does that help us?" asked Kali with a sneer.

"Because through their employment records we were able to deduce that they attacked us to get to Robyn," said Fan.

Eubule tensed in his chair.

"They've employed twenty fertility doctors in the last thirty years alone. When we looked into the records of the doctors, we found every one of them died or disappeared within six months of being let go. More than one died on the job."

Eubule noticeably tensed. Briton tried to put a hand on his shoulder but he shrugged it off.

"These people have secrets and they aren't above killing to keep them," said a vampire from their Japanese castle.

"Exactly. Robyn was pregnant at the time of her abduction," said Fan.

Many on the screens took surprised breaths. Anca hadn't realized that was something that wasn't widely known already.

That man from the Japanese castle spoke again. "Have strength, Eubule."

Eubule gave a tense nod.

Briton's daughter looked at her lap and stood up quickly. She took Fan's place without looking at her, her gaze focused on the phone in her hand. She tucked a lock of her blond hair behind her ear. "I just got word. We had agents in the library in the states." She gave Veia an uncertain look. Asking permission to go on with her eyes. Veia nodded, as did Briton and Eubule. "There are financial records connecting the church with an old brotherhood now located in Northeast Turkey --"

"Excellent, when do we leave?" said Trig.

"Trygve, our species may be at risk here. We cannot rush ahead blindly," Veia said this gently, but firmly. Trig gave a reluctant nod. Veia waved a hand at Cleona to continue. Briton gave her an encouraging smile.

Cleona returned her dad's smile and continued. "Formerly called the Aydinlatma Brotherhood, they now call themselves the Kuvvetli Guild. Every couple hundred years their name changes, making them fit our MO."

"Where did this information come from?" It was the vampire sitting across from Anca.

"We had a team sent to the states to check out the main office of the church. Through good field work and some hacking, they were able to recover financial records firmly connecting the church with the brotherhood. The rest we Googled. There isn't much room for secrets anymore," said Cleona.

Fan motioned to Cleona, who sat down next to her father. Fan stood up looking excited. "More information was found on the microchip. We had assumed, with our attackers likely being vampires, that they would have an antidote as a safeguard for themselves. We were right. According to the chip this, what we now know to be brotherhood has an antidote at their headquarters."

"Which is…?" said Kali.

"In Turkey, as Cleona just told us."

"Do we leave now?" asked Trig.

"Soon," said Fan. "Those fit enough to fight ship out tomorrow." She looked at the screens at the other councils around the world. "Any aid given could mean the difference between extinction and survival." She wasn't begging. She was making it perfectly clear that anyone that held back, even a single person, could make a difference.

"You have our aid," said a werewolf, and the others nodded.

"We pledge our soldiers and dragons," said the Japanese council.

One after another, each council promised to do all they could to help them win this fight. Anca nodded slowly. She had recommitted to becoming a soldier, and never had the stakes been higher.

CHAPTER 17

Anca left the meeting feeling extremely nervous yet oddly calm at the same time. She supposed it came from finally having a plan while facing down possible extinction. Her walking slowed.

"What is it?" asked Nuru.

"I just realized I might die soon. You could die." With all her attention on finding who to attack the news that everyone less than an Ancient could die hadn't properly sunk in.

Nuru pulled her into a hug as unbeckoned tears fell down her face.

"No matter what happens, I'm with you," said Nuru. "I'm here; draw on that."

She did. She concentrated on feeling him, his arms wrapped around her shoulders, his hands stroking her hair, how his waist felt beneath her arms. She pulled back to look him in the face. "I'm so glad I have you for this."

"And I'm glad I have you. You saved my life at The Gathering. I haven't forgotten."

"Does that mean you owe me?" She wiggled her eyebrows at him.

He nodded and smiled. "Yes, very much. I should probably start working on making it up to you right now." He began to pull her down the hall toward their room.

Fan was in front of them and waved at Anca wildly.

"I should see what she has to say. It could be important." *Stupid extinction, delaying my getting laid.*

"You're right. I'll be waiting." He said in a low voice before kissing her neck and leaving.

"Anca, comment ça va?"

"Pauvre."

"I suppose that was a silly question. My apologies. And not just for that, I seem to have interrupted something."

"It can wait, just not too long."

"Compris." Fan always switched between English and French when her and Anca talked. They had crossed paths many times at the compound. They weren't fast friends, but they were friendly enough with one another. "You've all been through much in the last week."

"Yeah, we have. One week. On se sent tellement plus longtemps," said Anca.

Fan touched her arm.

"I'm sorry you weren't told. Vraiment. We weren't allowed to tell anyone." Fan said.

"Well the secret is out now." Anca gestured behind them to the council meeting they'd just left.

Fan nodded and smiled. "I never thought anything of substance would come from my assignment. I thought they were just keeping me busy."

"Why would they want to keep you busy?"

Fan gave her a look.

"Right, you dated a werewolf," said Anca.

"As much as The Ancients preach tolerance, my dating Kurt was never smiled upon. The werewolves are slightly more tolerant, but as soon as we broke up, he was shipped off to Scotland."

"Half a world away from you at the time," said Anca with understanding.

"I know what a burden it is to be separated from the one you love. I requested Nuru come with us tomorrow. He'll be an asset. He can aid the witches with controlling the creatures. The Ancients insisted he stay outside during the attack."

Anca wasn't quite sure how to feel. She was happy that she'd have Nuru with her up until the attack, but she'd also be fretting about his safety the whole time. Telling him to stay outside could help but she knew if things started to get out of control Nuru would jump in. She also realized what she said was true, he'd be an asset to the witches. She couldn't ask them to keep him out of the fight for her peace of mind.

Anca nodded. "Thank you."

"We all leave in the morning for Turkey. Au revoir."

"Bye."

Anca headed toward her room. Maybe she could convince Urian to keep an eye on Nuru during the attack. She knew the odds of Urian actually being able to stop Nuru should he decide to jump into the fight were slim, but maybe he could at least give her a heads up should Nuru decide to do something stupid.

She opened the door to find Nuru on the bed, naked and clearly happy to see her. She gave him a wicked grin before closing the door and taking off her shirt.

CHAPTER 18

They boarded a plane for Turkey the next morning. More vampires would be joining them within a day of their arrival from around the world including France, the United States, Nigeria, Japan, and Bolivia. With everything that was a stake, they weren't going to hold back. Their best operatives were flying in.

Lita had insisted on coming with even though she wasn't too much of a fighter. "You need every soldier you can get." No one could argue so she was sitting across from Nuru on the flight much like she had on their flight to The Gathering. She wasn't giving Anca accusing stares this time, at least. She wasn't looking at much of anything: she was in her own world of worry. She and Anca had a weepy conversation before boarding. They were allowed the tears they'd decided, as they might die soon.

They didn't get a chance to relax on the flight. Surveillance pictures were sent to them along with records. Anca pulled up short as she held an older photograph of the members. Her heart stopped completely when she saw a surveillance photo that had been taken not two hours ago. She held up the black and white photograph next to the screen. "No. That's not possible."

"What's wrong?" Nuru was by her side, he lifted his head to look at the photos that held her attention so acutely.

"I think that's... but it can't be..." She placed the photograph on the table, switched the screen to a financial records file. "Nothing, I'm just imagining things."

A car was waiting for them in Turkey and... "Ode!" Anca dropped her bag and ran into her arms.

"Hey girl." Ode nearly picked her up. "Lita." Lita came forward for a hug as well. "Watch the hands." Lita backed away, hands raised, a smile on her face.

"I had to check you were real." Lita's face looked thoroughly unapologetic.

They were taken to a grand building of classical Turkish design in the city. The green roof and gold detailing would have looked garish if done improperly but here the effect was elegant and impressive. Zafir greeted them at the door.

He wore robes of sapphire blue, his black curls tousled in an effortless way that made him look lovely, not disheveled. A black beard was artfully trimmed, giving him a look of professionalism. His dark eyes shone with gratitude. "Hoş galindiz!" He spread his arms wide in welcome. He stepped forward to clasp forearms with Trig, an old warrior greeting. Next to Trig's large muscled frame, Zafir's lean five-foot four frame looked tiny. "I wish we were meeting under better circumstances old friend. I would invite you to falcon with me. It has been too long, but this must be dealt with swiftly. Those that harm our family must learn that to do so is a mistake."

"Couldn't agree more," said Trig.

They were led to feeders before they settled around a low table in a room where they took tea and were told what to do next. A small ferret-looking creature curled against Anca's back.

"With what we've gathered, it looks like this organization is not only old but influential. Many key members of the government are in their pocket. They have tread most carefully to stay under the radar," said Zafir.

"And you've found all this out in just a day?" Anca couldn't help but be impressed. She scratched the head of the creature curled against her.

"Things have changed Anca. Information is readily available. It is getting harder to keep secrets." His unspoken message that it was also getting harder for vampires to stay secret hung in the air. Zafir was in favor of vampires outing themselves before someone else could. It was easy to tell that in light of the recent attack, his opinion on this had only hardened. "A few of our field operatives are going to get a closer look at their office. A couple are watching some employees. One is tailing their vice president; he should be able to get us some valuable information by day's end." With that they were dismissed.

Nuru walked off to convene with the witches. Lita and Ode were off helping with office work. Trig and the others were discussing possible strategies. Anca felt like a proper bath.

A Turkish bath is a wonderous thing. Anca let her towel drop next to a white pillar. Her foot pierced the steaming water to set on the green and blue tiled step below its surface. She sank slowly into the round bathing pool that could have comfortably seated ten. With a possible fight ahead, she was forcing herself not to feel guilty about taking care of herself.

She sank lower in the water until her nose hovered just above the surface. She realized that this was the first time she'd been properly alone in days. It had been reassuring, after the chaos of The Gathering and what followed, to convince herself of the safety of her loved ones by keeping herself surrounded by them.

She gazed up at the green scale tiles covering the walls, imagining herself to be surrounded by a great coiled snake. *A bit like myself*, she realized. Coiled, ready to strike.

She soaked in the hot water for some time before her phone buzzed on a bench against the wall. She walked over to it, dripping water on the intricate tiling.

There was a message from Lita. We're needed. Room where we took tea. Five minutes. She set down the phone. Water dripped from her hands as she curled them into fists. Soon she could take on those that thought they could hurt her family. Her face hardened. Her eyes darkened.

More vampires had arrived with different creatures that they had agreed would be helpful with their attack. No greetings were being shared. Everyone was still, focused. All attention on their leaders for this mission.

"For those that weren't watching the council meeting, I will give a refresher. We found some of their financial records, employees specifically," said Fan. "They've employed virologists and fertility doctors for decades. We think they attacked us to get to Robyn and infect the rest of us. We also believe they have a cure or at least a treatment in the facility we are about to attack. We aren't positive about much else about the place. We don't know how many men are waiting for us, if they are predominately vampire, if they have creatures like we do, or what their defenses are. What we do know is if we don't act, most of us will be dead in ten days."

A group of werewolves entered the room. They seemed a bit apprehensive, as though they weren't sure how to act in the presence of so many vampires. Relations were good between the two species, but it had never been forgotten that they'd joined together for survival, not friendship. Anca noticed Fan stiffen and saw one of the werewolves quickly look away.

"One of our field agents is already tailing a virologist. We're going to bring him in. See what we can learn from him, offer our protection," said Zafir.

"Why would he want our protection?" asked one of the werewolves.

Fan looked at her. "Because everyone that has held that position before him has either disappeared or wound up dead."

Ode nodded solemnly. A golden drake curled around her shoulder with its tail flicking. They both seemed anxious to fight.

The werewolves eyed the drake. They weren't used to being around magical creatures.

"Where is this place exactly? Where we're attacking." asked Ode.

"Oldest building in the city. Three blocks from here," said Fan. "But we aren't moving in until we know more."

Trig and Lita spoke at the same time. "How much more do we need to know?" said Trig.

"What *else* do we need to know?" asked Lita.

"For one we don't know how many people may be waiting for us in there, we don't know if they are prepared for us, we don't know if they have The Ancients held hostage." Zafir's voice grew more agitated with each word.

"Our tempers are short," said Nuru. They all looked at him. "We need to go in smart or our own mistakes will defeat us. If they do have The Ancients, they could be set to kill them as soon as we bust down the door. Fan's right, we need to know more."

Anca hated to admit it, but he was right.

"They should be bringing in the virologist within the next…" Zafir looked at his watch, "Eighty minutes. Can we hold on until then?"

"I guess," said Trig stiffly. Lita nodded with the others.

They stood about the room in restless silence. The golden drake amused itself by roasting hazelnuts that Ode threw in the air. At one-point Tria asked for silence when Lita strummed her fingers against a table. Beyond that, they hovered, simply being until action could be taken. They didn't have to wait long.

The double doors to the tea room burst open. A confident face jeweled with smoldering eyes and edged with a strong jaw topped an athletic, well dressed body. In a voice rich as chocolate, Baris spoke. "My loves, I present Ted." He led the quivering soul into the room. He promptly collapsed in fear. "A gift for the queen of secrets." Stepping up to Fan, he gently pressed his lips to the knuckles of her hand. One of the werewolves clenched his jaw.

"Merci." She looked at the crowd and waved at the door. They didn't want to overwhelm the man. She turned to the man. "Ted was it?"

The man on the floor seemed moments away from wetting himself. He stared at the drake now curling itself around one of Ode's legs in disbelief. More brain than brawn clearly, but would he know what they needed?

"Why did you take me? What's going on? Who are you? What the hell is that?"

"We are here to help you." Fan sunk to her knees next to him. When Ode left the room with the drake, most of the people in the room followed. "We would like to offer you protection in exchange for information about the people you work for. We think they are planning to hurt you. You are a virologist, yes?"

"Yes." He calmed slightly at the ease of the question. This man probably identified as a virologist before anything else. People calm in the presence of familiarity.

"Were you aware that every virologist employed by these people before you have gone missing or been found dead?" asked Fan calmly.

He stilled. "I suspected." His voice barely a whisper, his gaze becoming unfocused. He rubbed his plump arms in an attempt to sooth himself. Tears threatened to well over his lashes to spill onto his face.

"That makes you very observant. Something we need." Fan held out a hand, offering to help him up. He took it. "We would like to know what you observed at work."

The man stood with Fan. "Perhaps more than I should have," he admitted.

"What is your job specifically?" she asked.

"I study a virus. A unique virus. I've never seen anything quite like it. It is quite the puzzle, but I'm beginning to reach the end of my abilities. They also asked me to create a *new* virus. One that would attack the one I'm studying. But they didn't give us enough time. They wanted it to kill, but we didn't have time."

"It killed plenty." Trig's voice came out growl. Fan gave him a scolding look. They needed this man to talk.

"You designed the counter virus?" asked Fan.

"Yes, I asked for more time, but they said the deadline couldn't be moved."

"Did you make a cure? A treatment?" asked Fan.

"Of course." He said it as though question was ridiculous. "They insisted on not keeping it in the lab though. I'm not sure why. I asked about it this morning, and he didn't seem happy. He said I was asking too many questions."

"I probably snagged you just in time," said Baris, leaning effortlessly against a wall. "More likely than not, there are men waiting for you at your home to kill you."

Ted looked stricken, but not shocked. As if Baris had exposed a truth he had hoped would turn out to be false but had known to be true.

Meryem sat up straight. "Could you recreate the cure?"

The entire room looked at the man.

"Not from memory. I'd need my notes or at the very least a sample of the cure so I could replicate it."

Anca's heart swelled. They just needed his notes or a sample. They could do that. They would.

Ted spoke. "I was asked, not long ago, if the virus could be strengthened."

Anca leaned forward. "Strengthened? How?"

"That's what I was trying to figure out. I thought maybe if two infected hosts mated, the resulting child would have a stronger version of the virus. That perhaps the virus evolved through the generations.. I told them it was possible, probable even.." Ted had begun ringing his hands, his shocked stillness turning to jittery nerves.

Fan touched his arm. "Was there any indication that they had procured such hosts?"

"Yes, I was told yesterday that I would have new samples from two such hosts. The mother and the produced offspring."

"So, they have them." Fan's arm dropped. She thought a moment. "Where are they keeping them? At the lab where you work?"

"No, that's the bit I shouldn't know. The samples took hours between my requests and their arrival. The guard muttered something once when he was leaving, I don't think he thought I could hear him. He said he hated driving to the Guild in mid-day traffic."

"So, you think that the hosts are being held at this Guild?"

"I remember because I thought it peculiar to keep specimens in, what I imagine to be, an office."

Fan nodded. "We know this guild. They own the lab you work for. The building's not far from here. Thank you for what you have told us. You have helped us save lives, yours included." She motioned to Baris, and the two of them led the man out of the room.

"We gather ourselves and attack as soon as we're ready," said Zafir as soon as they were out of the room. "But we won't be going in halfcocked. If The Ancients are in there, we can't risk being outnumbered or outgunned."

"Agreed," said Trig, Anca and Meryem.

Soon the rest of the arriving vampires were all gathered together. Weapons and creatures were being prepared for the fight. Drakes from China and Gryphons from France had arrived. An ogre was being kept in one of their more secure rooms; it would be held back until it was decided they needed it. When it got angry it was just as likely to attack them as who they were fighting.

It was decided they would attack just before first light. If there were younger vampires, they'd be settling in for the day, making them more likely to be caught off guard. It meant their own young vampires couldn't come, not that most of them could anyway with the state they were in, but they had agreed that they should attack soon. It was hard to kill an Ancient but not impossible. Every passing day increased the likelihood one of them was already dead.

Meryem had gone to stake out the Kuvvetli Guild's building. She called in at two in the morning. "We've found a way in."

"How?" asked Zafir.

"The front door. If we do this right, they should be dead before they know what hit them."

"Should?" Anca didn't like the sound of that but knew in operations like this surety was a rarity.

Zafir's face was serious. "Tell us what we need to do."

Two hours later Anca was getting herself mentally prepared for the fight ahead by walking around and looking at the other vampires.

This is what we're fighting for.

No matter how many times she'd been in a fight it was always the before she hated most. During the fighting, instincts and training took over. Before, there was only nerves and worry.

She was pacing up and down a hallway when she heard someone take a deep raged breath. She knew that noise, but she'd never heard it so distressed before. She walked toward the noise and knocked gently on the door.

"Trig let me in."

She didn't hear him protest, so she turned the handle. She opened the door to find Trig in a small study sitting on a wooden chair staring fixedly at the floor. His eyes were red, and he kept twisting his hands together.

"How..?" he choked.

Anca crouched on the floor in front of him. "It wasn't your fault."

"What -- What kind of man let's that --"

"You didn't let that happen. You were heavily drugged. Even The Ancients were knocked out. Even with all that in your veins, you were still fighting." Anca desperately wanted to reach out to him, but centuries together had taught Anca that Trig didn't want to be touched in moments like this.

"I should've..."

"There was nothing you could have done."

Trig refused to look her in the eye. "I could've fought harder."

"You did fight. Even when others were knocked out, you were still fighting."

Finally, he looked at her. "Derya."

"She was trying to save me. She thought she would heal or that I wouldn't... maybe both. We'll never know."

Trig looked away. "If I hadn't been... I could have protected her." A tear threatened to roll down his cheek.

Anca grabbed his face with both hands. "The fault of this lies squarely on the shoulders of those that attacked us. They are at fault. They are the ones that must pay, and we are the ones that will make them do so."

Trig looked her in the eyes and nodded.

When they rejoined the group, everyone was in full body armor and armed to the teeth, literally. Some of the younger vampires had metal fanged, Anca believed the term was. Grills. A few were even diamond tipped, a sure way to pierce through armor to get to delicate arteries.

Anca took a breath, tracing her hand around the Raging bull 454 she had strapped to her thigh. She nodded at Trig. "You ready for this?"

A gryphon was lying down next to a rack of different swords. It could sense the tension around it. It kept rearranging its wings.

Trig gave her a crooked grin. "A Viking is always ready for Valhalla."

"How silly of me to even ask," said Anca.

He turned back to loading bullets into his magazines.

Zafir appeared in the doorway. "Okay, it's time."

Anca grabbed her khopesh from the sword rack. It was a modern version of the Egyptian weapon she had on her mantle. It was two-feet long and curved. Other than her long nose and tanned skin, it was the only thing she had of her true father. She remembered the story her mother had told her about him. That her husband had been reported dead when Anca's father arrived looking to establish trade routes. After weeks of negotiation, he had left thinking the only thing he had left behind was the khopesh. When Anca's mother realized she was pregnant, she tried to find out what happened to him. She was told that he had been killed by the snow of the mountains, their bodies found frozen. Distraught that she would have to raise two children by two men alone, Anca's mother thought of ending the pregnancy. A day later her husband arrived, weak from his glance with death. He had survived the battle but only just. She quickly bedded her husband. For years, she insisted Anca was his. No one said they disbelieved her, and she often had Anca play in the sun, an excuse for her tanned skin.

Anca confronted her mother when she was six. She knew she was different from her brothers. She could see in her father's eyes that she didn't belong to him, that he knew she wasn't his. She wanted to know the secret of her past.

Years later, her mother confessed, giving her the khopesh as she told her everything. Anca had practiced with it at night when no one could see. Anca and her mother had never spoken of her true father again after that night.

She and Trig shared a steely look. She snapped the weapon into its sheath strapped diagonally across her back. For better or worse, this ended now.

CHAPTER 19

The building looked quiet, but that wasn't a surprise. Anca suspected even hell's gates would be silent until you opened them. That could well be what they were about to walk into.

The building was on the edge of the city, pushed up against the mountains. They made a perimeter behind the bushes struggling to grow out of the rock face. They watched the building. It was normal enough, but their knowledge of what lay inside made it ominous. Several windows shone with pale light. Could be a worker that had nothing better to do. Could be security. They'd assume the latter.

Meryem's team was going to head the charge, but that would come later. A strained whisper came across their earpieces.

"Releasing scout one."

Anca saw a tiny piece of shadow that was darker than the surrounding shadow. A flying ferret fitted with a camera was making its way toward the building. All around Anca witched were sitting cross-legged, eyes turned gold, giving slight nudges to the desires of the creatures, making them want to investigate the building. The shadow climbed a tall tree then took a great leap to the roof of the building. Anca saw what looked like an elongated flying squirrel sail through the air and land silently on the roof.

A werewolf nearby gave a confused look. He and Anca locked eyes for a moment. She gave him what she hoped was a reassuring nod. They'd been given a brief explanation of what to expect. They hadn't had much time to explain everything, so the werewolves would hang back slightly. They'd be one of the last waves, so they could learn as they went. Anca saw another vampire whispering hurriedly into another werewolf's ear. No doubt trying to tell her everything he could in what little time they had before they had to spring into action.

The voice came through their earpieces sounding slightly relieved. "Scout has reached target. Roof is either void of sensors, the creature is too small to set them off, or it is a silent alarm. Stand by."

A moment later a man appeared on the roof. He was silhouetted by the light of the open door. "Silent alarm it is. Reposition scout one."

Anca saw the long shadow shimmy down the side of the building. It worked a small window open and slithered inside. The man on the roof walked around a moment looking bored even at such a distance. He went inside, the roof going dark when he closed the door. A light appeared in the room the ferret had entered. The same man from the roof looked around then left the room, turning the light off behind him.

One question was answered. The building wasn't swarming with people, if it was it would have been a different man that searched the room. They were short staffed tonight.

"Visual ready."

Anca adjusted the shotgun hanging from her chest by a weapons retention device. She slid the O.D. socket in place and flicked the locking lever switch down. She turned on a small screen strapped to her forearm. The screen would have appeared as if it were on but that there was no image to a human. The brightness of the screen had been turned down as far as it could go. Anca and the other vampires could see what was on the screen just fine. All around eyes were glued to their own darkened screens and they watched the jumpy video that was being transmitted from the ferret's camera.

"Okay, send in the rest."

Over a dozen small shadows of different shapes moved down the rockface toward the building. Anca watched as one of her gryphons landed on the roof. *Stay safe.* She turned back to the screen on her arm. She tapped the screen in a three two pattern. Sections of screen folded out expanding the image. She tapped a few icons so she could watch four different feeds simultaneously. She watched the gryphon make its way through a small kitchen, distracted a moment by muffins on the counter before moving into the hallway. The ferret had made its way through the small window into a thickly carpeted office. The third screen showed the progress of a fruit dragon moving past a meeting room into a neighboring break room. The last screen was strapped to a fairy that had entered in to a bathroom, it was currently enjoying its reflection in the mirror. A moment later the fairy shook its head and flew out of the bathroom. A witch had just nudged her into being bored with her reflection, not an easy thing. Anca watched the screens as the creatures slunk from room to room, searching the entire building.

"Team one ready?"

"Ready."

"Go now."

Anca's heart clenched. She was part of the second team. She gripped her shotgun and took deep breaths.

On her screen she saw flashes of light. Muzzle flash. The team was clearing the building. She heard Meryem's voice, "Level one clear. Ready team two."

"Ready."

Anca exhaled. She shut her humanity off for the next several minutes. She was nothing more than a soldier. A hand was placed on her shoulder, she placed her hand on Trig's shoulder. He advanced toward the building, Tria flanking him.

Anca and the two others crouched on either side of the door. Tria nodded. Trig moved in followed by Tria then Anca. They immediately crouched in a similar formation as they had outside inside the building. Tad entered after them with one of his dragons. The dragon was acting much like a dog in a K-9 unit. It stayed at Tad's side, its head level with his hip.

Tad and the dragon took point. Vampire's senses were heightened but a dragon's sense of smell was still far superior. He crept forward with the dragon, making a thorough sweep of every corner and possible cover before advancing into the next room on their way to meet up with the first team. These floors had already been cleared but in these kinds of situations you assume nothing especially when the enemy may be excepting you.

"Level two clear." Came through the earpiece.

One more level to go.

They coordinated with the first team to simultaneously enter the third floor. Anca and her team were on the opposite side of the building waiting in a stairwell. She signaled with her hand for Trig to come forward while she held her position. He went past her and entered the first door. She heard a dull thud followed by a hollow crack. Trig's face popped back into view. He nodded, the room was now clear.

Anca kept herself from scolding him. This was not the time for him to prove he was lethal. They needed to question whoever they found. She moved forward.

If he has another power trip I'm going to have to talk to him.

Tadashi went next, dragon in toe. Anca heard a yelp of confusion. She felt a hand on her back, Tria signaling her to go forward. She went toward the noise. She waited just behind Tad in time to see the dragon leap over a half wall and latch onto the shoulder of a man that was on his way to a half open door. The dragon slammed him to the floor, his wings wrapped around the man's head to muffle his shouts. Tad was on him in a second.

"無料"Tad told the dragon. The dragon let go. Tad nodded to Anca, "We need information."

"Of course." Anca heard Trig informing the others that they had found someone. She kneeled next to the man. "Tell me about your security."

The man spat in her face.

She wiped it off slowly. "Okay, let me rephrase." She took her boot knife from her right leg and put it through the man's shoulder. He didn't scream but she could tell by his face that he was in pain. "Tell me," she twisted the knife, "about your security," she twisted the knife deeper, "or I let the dragon *eat* you."

The dragon growled, flame lighting up the back of its throat.

The man looked surprised. Anca wasn't, most people had never heard that threat before. He clenched his jaw.

"Tad," she said.

"火災" he said. The dragon covered the man's face with fire, Anca covered his mouth with her hand. The fire hurt but she'd heal. His face and her hand immediately covered in blisters.

Tria's head appeared through a doorway. "Hey, we don't need him." She went back into the room the man had been heading for.

Anca slit the man's throat so he couldn't make any noise before taking her hand away. Tad said something to the dragon. She heard crunching and gurgling noises.

"What did you find?" asked Anca.

"This is their security center for this part of the building," said Tria.

"This part?" Anca asked.

"Looks like there's some sort of basement," said Trig. "It doesn't even say where the entrance is."

"Well if we search the ground floor and there's space that should be there that isn't we know that that would be a path from the second floor to the basement. If we don't find anything like that then we search the first floor for an entryway," said Anca.

"Good, I'll tell the others." Tria tapped the microphone on her neck and relayed the information. "There's no uncalled-for space on the first floor according to the floor plans that were made with the footage from the scouts."

Anca tapped her own screen. Those that were still waiting at the perimeter had created a 3-D map of the building. She checked the first floor, no missing space. "Okay so we check the floors and the walls that are against the mountain."

Tria nodded. "Agreed."

Anca and some others wound up searching one of the offices that had a wall against the mountain.

Meryem spoke. "These guys are into some pretty dark stuff." She lifted a book up to show them the cover, *A History of Torture: The Best Methods*. Anca saw a spine that read, *Pain: The Great Divider*.

"Who are these people?" Tria muttered.

"I'm starting to have a theory…" said Zafir. "I just hope I'm wrong."

"What is it?" asked Tria.

"Books on torture and pain. An affinity for secrecy. Our biggest clue, the attack on us. I think they might be the Blood Brothers," said Zafir.

"You're right," said Anca, "I really hope you're wrong." *It wasn't him.*

"That would explain why The Ancients have been so secretive too. They consider them a blight on our history." Meryem looked at Zafir.

"But their supposed to be a myth. A vampire bedtime story about why you shouldn't stray from our family," said Zafir.

"They're supposed to be dead anyway." Everyone looked at Meryem with mild surprise. "We weren't supposed to talk about them, but I'm tired of keeping their secrets. It has cost us lives," Meryem said as she approached a new section of bookshelf.

Anca gave her a tense look. Zafir looked stunned.

Meryem spoke. "The Blood Brothers aren't a myth."

"Meryem," said Anca.

"I know you have your reasons for wanting to keep this secret, but we can't keep this quiet anymore," said Meryem.

"Enough, this is not the time. The clock is ticking. They may already know we're here. They could be killing The Ancients as we speak. If these people are the Blood Brothers you know very well they'll want The Ancients dead," Anca's breathing had become heavy. *What if he finds out? What if he is here?*

"She has a point," said Zafir. "Keep looking for a way in. Anything."

"Look at this." Meryem was handling a marble bust on the bookshelf. No matter how she yanked on it, it wouldn't budge. A slight seem could be seen at the base of the neck just above the collar. She tried pushing down on it, shoving the head back to expose a button, but there was none. Trig stepped forward, Meryem let him have a try.

"Love pain…" He twisted the head as if he meant to snap the figures neck. It moved. A book tilted forward one shelf down and to his right. He inspected it and pushed it back into place. A section of bookcase four feet wide opened against the outer wall. A thick wooden door with iron hinges lay behind it.

Everyone tensed.

"We found the entrance." Tria said into the microphone on her neck. Moments later the office was filled with vampires staring at the door.

Anca stepped forward, Tria right behind her. Anca poked the door with her rifle. Nothing happened. She gripped the handle. Hissing she drew her hand back. Everyone tightened their grips on their rifles.

"What happened?" asked Tria.

"Pricked my finger." The door gave a click. "Must open for vampires."

Zafir pushed past her, taking point. The staircase that was before them was narrow, just under three feet wide, a bottle neck. "I don't like this," he said.

"No one does," said Trig, giving a nod. Anca followed Meryem down into the unknown, Trig on her heels.

She heard Forrest radio the rest letting them know where they were going. He told one group to hold the building and the rest to follow them down. They'd leave a ladder of vampires behind them so they could get out if something went wrong.

They'd descended about forty feet when Zafir signaled for a halt. They had come upon an iron door with no lock. Zafir opened it slowly. Inside were various knives and chains. A chair with straps to hold its occupant in place.

"I know what this is," breathed Meryem.

"What?" whispered Anca.

"A cleansing room," said Zafir.

"They are the Blood Brothers," said Meryem. "They do still exist. But I thought..."

"Well, I'm glad we came fully armed then." Anca's heart quickened. She didn't have time to give everyone a history lesson. She thought back to her conversation with Veia and shook her head. So many secrets. If they were dealing with the Blood Brothers, and it was looking more and more like they were, then the repercussions could tear their family apart. That was a worry for another day. For now, Anca chose to concentrate on not dying.

Another thought occurred to Anca. If they were fighting the Blood Brothers, then the man she saw in the photographs was definitely... She pushed the thought away. *Deal with it later. If he is here you'll deal with it when and if you have to.* She clenched her jaw and kept going, her nerves on high alert.

Zafir spoke into his microphone. "Send down team four with their helpers."

They left the room and continued their descent. Slowly the brick walls turned to stone. Anca noticed the tool marks in the stone were worn smooth, as if they'd been exposed to centuries of pressing hands. This passage could easily be older than the city. How long had the Blood Brothers been here? Was this how'd they'd stayed hidden for the past three centuries? They stayed underground? It wouldn't just provide a hiding place, it would also protect them from the sun.

A large cavern opened up to their right up ahead. Zafir signaled for them to crawl over the walkway, keeping them out of sight. Stealth was still their most important weapon. Knowing they were going up against the Blood Brothers changed nothing. Anca repeated this to herself.

The passage forked. Zafir waited until the next group had joined them. Notifying those yet to join them. He had them split into two groups. He led his team left, Tria led her group right. Anca, Meryem and Trig went right.

Passing through the hallway like ghosts, they entered a chamber. It appeared to be a feeding area. Humans were kept in gibbets. Most were passed out, but one man saw them and began to beg for his life. Anca approached him, shotgun down, hands held up in surrender. "We're not going to hurt you."

"Please, enough. I've given enough." His voice was weak, desperate.

"We're here to help." She approached slowly.

"No! No more!" His shouting was too loud, someone would hear. There was a chance someone would hear him and think it was just a brother getting a snack, but they couldn't afford the risk.

"Quiet him or I shoot," said Meryem.

"Sir, please --"

He screamed all the louder. "No! No, enough! Please!"

Footsteps were making their way toward them. "Too late," said Meryem.

A shirtless man appeared in a doorway on the other side of the room. Pale scars covered his chest suggesting he'd endured a level of pain his enemies wouldn't think to inflict on another person. Anca had only to look at those scars and see the lack of any kindness in his eyes to know: he was a Blood Brother. She forced herself not to panic.

Surprise showed briefly on his face, but it didn't cause him to hesitate. He took the knife strapped to his thigh and threw it. The knife grazed Anca's shoulder. Trig shot at the man but he dodged the attack. He slammed the door shut, taking two more bullets to his back. Anca heard a deadbolt snap. The man went to the caged man, kicked the gibbet, the man screamed in panic. The other humans woke up screaming, begging for their lives. The Blood Brother continued to dodge their attacks all the while kicking the gibbets causing the humans to scream all the louder. The door was shut, momentarily trapping them in the room and with the humans screaming their element of surprise was slipping away.

Trig stepped forward and began punching every inch of the man he could reach.

"Trig get down!" Anca shouted.

Trig ignored her and kept wailing on the man receiving numerous blows himself.

"That's it," Anca muttered. She shot Trig in the shoulder.

He turned toward her, a stunned look on his face. The man behind him finally had his face fully exposed. She put the rest of her clip into his head.

Trig looked at her with indignancy. "You shot me!"

Anca stepped up to him and punched him in the face. "This is not the time for you to doubt yourself.

This is exactly what they wanted for you to think, that you earned that. You didn't: *no one* earns that. They were threatened by you and for good reason. You are one of the baddest motherfuckers I know, that I have ever known. You could tear this place apart by yourself but not if you keep trying to prove how tough you are!"

Trig stared at her. He was breathing heavy and looked like he might attack her.

"Unleash yourself on them!" Anca pointed toward the door the man had come through. The sounds of men waking, running and shouting alerts were coming from behind it.

Trig looked at the man dead on the floor. He spared a brief glance to the humans in the gibbets that were screaming. He took a deep breath and looked at Anca. "I'm sorry."

"I don't need you to be sorry. I need you to be pissed at the right people."

He nodded and positioned himself to attack the door. "Let's do this."

CHAPTER 20

"Anca! Door!"

Anca walked over the body she had made short work of to the door, actively ignoring the bodies in the gibbets. She pressed the muzzle of her shotgun against the door where the deadbolt was. She looked at Meryem, who nodded. Anca fired at a forty-five-degree downward angle then turned so she was facing away from the door and kicked it open. She sprinted a few steps, crouched and spun to cover the door.

They could hear footsteps. "Grenade." Trig lobbed the weapon down the hallway. Anca didn't move even after the dust from the explosion had settled. In these kinds of situations, you didn't move until you were told.

Meryem went through the door crouching just inside it. Trig entered from the left, crouching on the right side opposite Meryem.

"Ready," said Meryem.

Anca went in. She moved fast over the body parts down the hallway. There was a hallway to the left. She acted on a hunch and reattached the shotgun to her chest taking her khopesh out. She saw a shadow on the floor indicating there was someone around the corner. She flicked a small piece of rubble down the hall. The man advanced straight ahead just enough that the muzzle was visible. Anca acted.

The khopesh is curved. Near the end of the blade on the dull side there is a slight hook. Usually this is used to hook another blade and knock it out of the way. Anca had discovered this small feature could be useful against handguns as well. She hooked the pistol and pulled it out of the man's hands, keeping the momentum of the strike going she twirled the sword and struck down against the man's arm.

There was a wet slap as the man's arm hit the floor. He looked surprised, the pain not yet registering when Anca sunk her blade into his left shoulder. More men were behind him. Leaving her sword in the man's shoulder, she used him as a human shield lifting her shotgun and firing at the dozen oncoming men. There was some sort of cave at the end of the hallway beyond them. Anca pulled back going right. She pulled her sword out of the man's shoulder.

"Anca! Helpers!"

Her eyes widened. She gripped the man against her and retreated farther down the hallway. A drake the size of a man came barreling down the hallway, another dragon flying above it. She crouched lower, shielding more of herself with the body. Intense heat filled the hallway. She struggled to breath, choking on the boiling air. Her hand that had already healed from the burn from earlier blossomed with new boils. She screamed. She'd been burned by dragons before, but they had been displeased about a lack of treats or her infrequency of play time, their fire reached a ridiculous intensity when they were pissed off and looking for a kill.

Screams echoed off the walls of the hallway into Anca's ears. She dropped the body and advanced behind the dragons, sword raised. Trig made his way toward her, pistol at the ready. Anca had wondered at first why most of his pistols were fixed with suppressors. To a vampire's ears, they did almost nothing. Then she had fired one. The suppressor helped with the balance of the gun and reduced the upward recoil allowing for faster recovery. In a situation like this, vampire against vampire, every millisecond counted. Keeping that in mind, Anca sheathed her khopesh and brought up her Raging bull 454.

"Helpers," Tad said behind them. The dragons looked past Anca at him. "Free feed." The dragons sprinted off in glee.

They had made a point while they geared up that every dragon sniff each of them. Tad had just given them permission to eat anyone they didn't know. *I almost feel sorry for the bastards that run into them.*

They made their way past the hall with the burning bodies and continued down the hallway.

The hallway ended in a small balcony area that overlooked the cave. Trig settled in, his rifle up and ready. He started picking off men left and right.

"Tad and I will stay with Trig. You go back and direct the others," said Meryem.

Anca nodded and headed back up the hallway. She had just entered the feeding room when, across the room, the next team appeared. She held her hands up to avoid getting shot. With so much adrenaline pumping, it was easy to shoot anything that moved.

She started to brief the new team on what had happened so far. "We split up --"

"We heard, so did we," said Forrest. Daran waved at her from behind him.

"Right, of course." *The walkie talkies we've been talking into. I've been out of the field for so long.*

"What helpers are this way?"

"A drake, a dragon and Tad's small dragon. He gave the first two free reign already."

"Poor bastards." Forrest signaled to his team. Anca fell in line, advancing with the others. A moon priest stayed to hold the room. Anca saw him approach the bodies in the gibbets to offer a prayer for peace after their suffering. *I just hope we don't all need prayers by the end of this.*

Tria saw them approaching. "Can you spare Baris? No offense Trig but he's one of our best snipers and this spot is pretty prime."

"No offense taken." He fired again.

Anca smiled to herself. *I need to punch him in the face more often.*

Forrest nodded to Baris. He set up next to Trig and began firing. Trig left his position and joined Forrest and Anca. Tria stayed behind to cover Baris and Tad joined the rest of them.

Forrest gave them quick instruction as they made their way to the main cave. "It is unlikely that they are dressed in full tactical gear, but if you aren't sure if they're one of ours, shoot to incapacitate and opt for close up kills just to be sure." They passed through a double door into the main cave. It was chaos.

Anca immediately ducked, hauling Daran down with her. Another dragon flew overhead spewing flame at anything that moved. Daran got up. "Thanks, but I got this."

Daran was so elegant and adopted the speech of the times so quickly, Anca easily forgot how old he was. He was much older than her and far more powerful.

He gave the dragon's flame a calculative look then raised his arms high over his head. The flame began to swirl in the air. Daran lowered his arms, stretching them out in front of him. The swirling orb of fire lowered onto a group of Blood Brothers slightly to their left that had just entered the large cave. They weren't near anyone yet. Their screams joined the general cacophony.

The explosives Anca had strapped to her seemed to press against her on its own as she thought of her objective: kill the blood brothers, rescue The Ancients, find the cure, blow up everything else. She scanned the area as she shot at the Blood Brothers. Double doors ten feet high were open to her far left. If an explosive was planted there it would collapse the hallways they'd come in through possibly sealing in the Blood Brothers. They'd be buried, assuming there wasn't another exit, which there probably was. The loss of this exit would slow them down though and make escape more difficult and immeasurably slower.

She took a deep breath. "Cover me." She fired as she ran for the doors. She opened them completely leaving only a foot of space between each door and the wall they were set in. She took her bricks of explosive and put half of them behind each door. She made a careful slit in the plastic casing and slowly pushed in the critical agent that turned the brick from harmless to lethal. She took a scan of the room before sliding in the pin, turning it on and sprinting away as fast as she could. *Please don't shoot, please don't shoot.* She did not want to be close when that went off.

It looked like their plan of attacking just before sunrise had worked. The Blood Brothers kept coming at them, but some of them were attacking without weapons still half asleep. That didn't make it an easy fight. The Blood Brothers were used to pain. Where Anca could take several bullets and keep fighting, it took two full clips before these guys stopped attacking.

The werewolves had thrown them off, at least. They seemed surprised to see the vampires and werewolves fighting side by side. The priestesses were also a shock. The clang of chains rang through the cavern. The Blood Brothers seemed to have been expecting the dragons, as some of the Blood Brothers used their being set on fire as a weapon.

One such man was coming at Anca. Half his body was on fire. Anca put four shells in him, shooting a line across his abdomen. He merely leered at her until she thrust her arm through the tattered hole up into his chest cavity, ripping out his heart. She unsheathed her khopesh and cut off his head. His confused expression rolled across the floor. Trig came to her side and patted out the flame that was spreading across her front.

"Fifl." He muttered.

She gave him a look and saw a man taking aim behind him. She shoved Trig down, drew and fired her pistol dodging the man's first two bullets. She hit him in the head twice. No matter how fast you healed, a 44 magnum to the head was going to put you out of commission for a while.

"Reload," she said.

Trig got up into a crouch to give her cover as she reloaded her shotgun and pistol.

"Good!" She swung up and fired at a Blood Brother that had been running at them to her left. She fired again at the man that had replaced him. A werewolf in full form came out of nowhere and grabbed the man around the middle slamming him bodily to the floor. He lashed at his chest with his massive claws until the skin tore away. Anca ran up to help decapitate the vampire as the werewolf's clawed hand reemerged from the mangled chest with a shredded heart.

Glad those razor claws are on our side.

A drake had climbed a wall to their right and was now snacking on one of the Blood Brothers that had been shooting from the balcony. It dragged the body up onto the ceiling digging its claws into the rough rock. Another blood brother shot at the drake. It screamed as the bullets scraped its thick hide. There was a hollow cracking sound. Trig looked up in time to see the stalactite the drake had been clinging to come loose. He shouted. Anca dragged the werewolf after her and ran out of the way, firing as she went. The rock came crashing down not two feet from where they had been.

Anca lost track of Trig and focused on firing at anything that looked suspicious. The dragons were throwing flame everywhere; more than once she had to dodge to find cover. As the fight was becoming more intense, the dragons were getting less picky about who they scorched. Daran and a couple other witches were near the hallway they had entered from trying to control the flames as best they could to protect their own. They were drenched in sweat from the effort.

Anca saw a great jaguar made of white smoke leaping in from of Blood Brothers to block her fellow vampires from view. There weren't many witches that could do anything substantial. Briton could have dealt with the flame on his own, but they had agreed the surviving Ancients would stay behind. It wasn't worth risking what could be the last Ancients for an edge in this fight. If Anca and the rest died, at least vampires could begin again with two Ancients to guide them.

A great crashing sound filled the cave. Suddenly there was flame everywhere. She grabbed a passing werewolf and ducked behind one of the larger rocks that had fallen. She heard a roar that made her bones ache. The werewolf morphed enough back so a human face to look her in the eye with total confusion.

"Shit," said Anca. She looked over the rock. An ogre had come smashing through the hallway where the witches had been a moment before. *That explains the fire.* The witches' concentration would have broken trying not to get smashed by the ogre. *Gods I hope they're okay.* She knew this creature, if she could direct it to the Blood Brothers and keep out of its way...

They didn't exactly have a ton of root vegetables laying around. But there was plenty of charred meat and that gave her an idea. "Daran!" She broke cover and ran for Daran.

"Daran, can you affect the air currents so that the smell from a body makes it to the ogres nose?"

He nodded, a confused look on his face.

"Okay then." She grabbed a body off the floor and flung it into the air toward a group of blood brothers. "Now!" She felt the air ripple around her. The ogre's nostrils flared, and it went barreling after the meat and the Blood Brothers. They began firing at it, which only pissed it off.

"You know that gives me another idea. Tad!" He appeared at her side with his dragon as if he'd been waiting for her call. "Can we use your dragon?"

"Of course," he said.

"Daran, can you get this guy to shoot flame when I say?" He nodded. "Okay, here goes nothing." She grabbed another body off the floor and flung it into the air. "Now!" A stream of fire passed her and encased the body in flame. It hit the ground near a group of Blood Brothers. While they were trying to dodge the flame, Trig started firing. Headshots for everyone.

Others saw what they had done and began throwing flaming corpses as well. Tad ran off to lend his dragon to another group as Daran was redirecting existing flame to set alight corpses. The woman Anca had fought with during their escape from the lab was picking up corpses and electrocuting them until they smoked and then chucking them through the air. Anca ran toward the Blood Brothers as they tried to fight the sudden onslaught of raining corpses, chopping heads as she went. With the new strategy, Anca felt the fight begin to slowly swing in their favor.

The werewolves were steering clear of all the flame or turning back to human form so their fur didn't catch on fire. The Blood Brothers had too much to dodge at once. Flaming bodies, dragons, werewolves, a pissed off ogre, smoke creatures, and highly trained vampires would be too much for almost anyone. But they weren't just anyone.

Anca was able to see a man in a suit run into a tunnel after she'd relieved a Blood Brother of his head. She ran after him, her instincts screaming *threat*.

The long tunnel was surprisingly new. She didn't see the man as she ran down the hall, her footfalls echoing hollowly. There was a set of white metal doors with reinforced glass windows like you might see at a hospital or prison. She kicked them in, her gun raised.

The man was facing away from her frantically pressing buttons. There was a large screen level with his head. He was taking a conference call. She heard a woman's voice: "Enough of the traitors have been moved. Eliminate the rest. They must not know --" The woman's gaze locked onto Anca, and the screen went black. She took aim between the large columns of the room and shot the man twice in the neck.

He fell into a pool of his own blood. He gave her a sideways glance. "I thought you retired." He turned himself onto his back. He looked at odds with his surroundings. His gelled hair spotted with blood. His white shirt now stained with red.

She knew him.

She looked at the face she'd seen in the pictures on the plane, the face she thought she'd seen the last of thirty centuries earlier. That face looked back at her in full.

"No! You're dead." She raised her gun more fully.

"Still alive Anca."

"Ioseph," she breathed.

"Hello, sister."

CHAPTER 21

"How…?" *What the fuck is going on?* Despite her shock she hadn't stopped being a soldier. She noticed that the columns were actually tanks. There were only ten and most of them were empty. Three of the tanks still held Ancients. There were also promising looking syringes on a counter.

"By being a vampire obviously," he said.

"I knew you were a vampire. Shut up." She pointed at the syringes. "Is that the cure?"

"How did you learn about the cure?"

So, that's a yes.

"It wasn't a fight over hunting territory that started the fight was it?" Get him talking, scan the room for more samples of the cure. The more they had the quicker it could be administered to those already sick. Every extra cure would be a life saved.

"That killed our village? No. The Blood Brothers wanted proof of my loyalty, so I convinced our neighbors that we would kill them in their sleep to ensure we had enough to make it through the winter. It didn't take much for them to start bashing each other's skulls in. Violence dances on the edge of every mind. We just don't pretend it doesn't."

"That's not true."

"Says the woman with a gun to my head."

"There's a gun to your head because you attacked my family."

"You attacked us."

"You attacked The Gathering."

"Did we?"

Don't let him get in your head.

"How are you still alive? No one was supposed to get out alive."

He faced her fully. "You knew?"

"I just found out."

"Yet you still fight with them?"

"They're my family," she said.

"So was I."

He leapt up taking her out at the knees. Her gun scuttered to a stop beneath one of the tanks. She brought her elbow down on the top of his head as they slammed into the wall.

He reached for one of her knives, but she blocked him just as his fingertips grazed the metal. Her block had left her side exposed, he punched, she felt a rib dislocate. She ignored it, it would heal in a minute but in the wrong place. He grabbed at her boot knife tucked in her left boot. She tucked her legs and launched him off her.

He recovered, quickly landing on his knees and running back toward her. He launched off the wall, altering his angle of attack. He came down hard stabbing her boot knife deep into her left shoulder. She turned her cry of pain into a war cry and headbutted him. She ripped out the knife and stabbed at his abdomen. He was unbalanced but only for a moment. She took the opening and sprinted toward her gun. She took the knife and, instead of throwing it at Iosef, sank it deep into the glass of one of the tanks, then fired her shotgun at one of the tanks.

There was a fogginess coming off The Ancients and the liquid was churning. The tubes connected to them were disintegrating. The liquid the remaining Ancients were suspended in was turning to acid. It was a desperate 'If we can't have them no one can' move. Every Ancient here was going to die if she didn't get them out fast.

She thought about her main objective and glanced at the counter that had the syringes on it. There were only three. Ioseph followed her gaze and made for the cures. She sprinted after him striking out at his legs making him stumble. If he broke even a single syringe…

He stumbled but didn't fall. He turned around and straight armed Anca. *It's like being charged by an elephant,* was her first thought. For a moment she was back in India fighting to extract Lahair.

She slammed into the ground like a high jumper. All of her breath left her, and she struggled to find it again. She gulped at the air, willing it to enter her lungs, trying to breath as she watched in horror as Ioseph smashed all three syringes.

She forced herself up. She could see her shotgun and grabbed it. A knee slammed into her back spilling her forward. She felt her cheek bone crack as she caught a glimpse of her gun on the floor, her shotgun spun away out of sight. She turned over just in time to avoid getting a fist to the same cheek that had just cracked. The cement floor next to her face cracked with the impact.

She flung her legs up and wrapped them around his right arm and head. He stood up and slammed her to the floor in an attempt to break her grip. She held on. He stood up and slammed her into the floor again and again. Her back was starting to ache. He stood up again. Anca unsheathed her khopesh and slashed at his lower torso. He backed up and slammed into one of the tanks, they broke their grips at the same time falling in a tangle of confusion.

She swung her khopesh hard, sinking it deep in his hip. He screamed, grabbing the sword to rip it out. Anca was already running away, toward her gun. She grabbed it and fired at three different tanks between her and Ioseph. He threw the sword at her and it stuck in the glass of one of the tanks behind her, then he screamed.

Anca scrambled off the floor, mortified by what she saw. The acid of the tanks was pouring out onto the floor. Iosef was flopping on the ground, his injured hip not healing fast enough to allow him to get off the floor in time. She climbed higher up on the tank and fired at every tank she could filling the floor with more acid.

Meryem appeared in the doorway.

"Stay back!" Anca warned her.

Meryem signaled a halt to the ones behind her out of Anca's sight.

After several minutes, a small drain in the floor did its job and funneled away all the acid on the floor. Meryem and the others approached cautiously, but quickly, working to get The Ancients out of the tanks and back to safety. Anca grabbed her brother by his remaining foot and dragged him out the hall.

"Anca!" Trig pulled her into a tight embrace, relief flooded his voice. He was standing with the others around a small group of hostages. She looked around and saw her fellow vampires patching themselves up, setting bones so they'd heal straight and popping joints back in place. The cuts would heal on their own. The werewolves were already leaving; they healed quicker and slower than vampires. The wounds would repair, but they'd need to rest, since they fatigued quicker. Everyone was sprayed with various amounts of blood. The priestesses were offering prayers to the fallen, some of them their own. The dragons were being coaxed out of the way and back to their cages waiting for them outside.

"You okay?" Trig asked.

She nodded, the exhaustion of fighting for so long was starting to surface. She fingered her hair. It had been burned at some point. *I'll need another haircut.* She glanced at her brother.

Trig saw her look at Iosef's body. Half of his face was melted away and slowly healing. Most of his right leg was gone. His eyes fluttered as he began to wake.

"Who's that?" Trig asked.

"My brother."

Trig's mouth fell open. He looked like a gasping fish. She placed a hand on his shoulder, smearing even more blood on his sleeve. "I'll explain later. First we need to figure out what to do with these guys." She nudged another captured Blood Brother with her toe.

"We should question them," said Zafir.

"How?" asked Fan. "They torture themselves for kicks. Nothing we do is going to crack them."

"Which leaves us with one choice." They turned to look at Anca. "Kill them all and hope there aren't more of them. Then scour the place for clues and blow up the rest as planned."

Iosef laughed through a mouthful of blood, the sliced skin under his ribs flapping comically. "I'm proud of you sister. You would have never made that call before."

"Things change," she growled.

"You choose a foolish path --" he started to say.

She leaned down so she was inches from his face. "I chose family and preservation. You chose blood and betrayal. Now you will burn for your choice."

CHAPTER 22

Isobella had insisted on taking blood from the captives before killing them. If they hadn't been able to find a cure, maybe Ted could extract it from their blood. It made sense. The Blood Brothers would have given themselves the cure before letting it lose in the world as a precaution. They loved pain, but they didn't have a death wish.

One of The Ancients' tanks hadn't been destroyed enough to let out all the acid. He was completely gone from the ribs down. The two that had survived had been removed immediately. They were to be sent to the castle in South America where they would heal and hide.

Nuru had come in to help with the injured and extract as much information as he could from the Blood Brothers that were still alive. Anca watched in fascination as his eyes glazed over as he touched his fingertips to their temples. When he approached Ioseph, he looked back at Anca with an extended hand. A question and an invitation.

She hesitated, then stepped forward. Nuru placed one hand against Ioseph's temple then the other to Anca's. Ioseph didn't struggle, not on the outside. To lookers on it would have appeared Nuru and Ioseph were trying to puzzle out a particularly difficult question. Inside there was a war going on. Nuru's mental powers slammed against a wall of resistance Ioseph had managed to throw up. After several minutes the wall cracked, but so did Nuru. He let his arms fall.

He looked Ioseph in the eye as he called for Daran. Much older, Daran was the best magick wielder they had with them. He stepped forward, eyes without mercy. It was a show of his ancient ferocity, one you didn't often see. He didn't break his gaze with Ioseph as he lifted a hand to his temple and Anca's.

The wall shattered.

Anca was standing in the building they had entered through. The office that held the entrance to the caves below was being fitted with the secret door. "You just grab the handle, and it will prick your finger. Genetic markers from each of you have been selected. Only someone who has those genetic markers *and* has the vampire virus can get through."

Anca felt Ioseph think of her then wave it aside. *She's retired. She won't come.*

Anca was standing in the mountains of Romania looking at her family three thousand years ago. It was nearly dark. She saw herself go out of their home and head for the tree she had hidden her khopesh in. She hadn't realized how bad she was at sneaking off. A moment later she saw Ioseph leave out of his bedroom window, a small sack slung over his back.

The scenery changed. Anca was standing in a small stone building looking at Ioseph smiling at an older man as he offered his arm. The older man ignored the arm and lunged at Ioseph's throat.

The building changed, aged. It looked older. Anca scanned the room and saw Ioseph smirking at the old man as he spoke. "Your village burns. None survived. Will you weep for them?" His voice was deep, saturated with age and knowledge.

"Never," said Ioseph.

Anca was looking at the room her and Ioseph had just fought in. Ancients were being removed. "You have your orders," said the woman from the screen. "This facility is nothing. We will take these traitors to join the rest. Destroy the cure. I told you it was foolish to place both in one area."

"We had no idea they would be able to get down here."

"Your failure has been noted. Enough of the traitors have been moved. Eliminate the rest. They must not know-" The scenery changed, and she tried not to be sick.

Ioseph was standing in a hallway, looking at a small glass room filled with dead babies. "I guess we need to wait until they procure one for us. This clearly isn't working." He nodded at another man in a suit who pressed a large button on the wall. The room filled with flame.

Ioseph was talking the human Anca had left in charge of the conservatory in France. "You're sure this is the schedule?" asked Ioseph.

"Absolutely, that's when they'll be at their weakest. The security measures are there as well," said the man.

"Good. You'll need to stay there. You need to pretend everything is normal."

The man looked stricken as his form faded to make way for the next scene.

Anca saw Ioseph standing behind Trig's sisters in a wooded area. He looked smug. "A gift. Perhaps this will push him to join our cause."

The girls whimpered. Their faces were covered in bruises. The old man that had attacked Ioseph in a previous vision gave Ioseph an appreciative smile. "You prove yourself once again." The man's face blurred as the scene shifted.

Anca stood in an office. Ted was sitting across from Ioseph. "We need more time. This virus won't be killed easily. We can harm it, but to kill it off completely…"

"The deadline cannot be moved," said Ioseph.

"About the other matter --"

"You ask too many questions about that. I would stop." Ioseph's threat was clear behind his smile.

The scenery changed again. She was watching Ioseph sign paperwork in a meeting room. "I'm sure you'll be pleased. I would bet my life on it." He smiled at the others around the table.

"Make no mistake, your life does depend on it."

Anca hurried to look at the paperwork. She saw Ioseph sign off on several experiments involving infants. They were trying to turn infants into vampires.

Anca was back in the cave, the fight in full force. She saw herself dart across the cave and set the explosives behind the door. Ioseph snapped the neck of a werewolf before dodging a flaming corpse. He heard a command come through his earpiece telling him to assist in the evacuation of the traitors. He fought his way around the ogre to get to the holding room.

Anca stood in a meeting room. Ioseph was at the end of a long table, clearly the least important person there.

An older woman near the top of the table spoke. "This Trygve has been researching *fake* blood," she spat the words. "It is an insult. He must be dealt with. His body needs to hang where it can be seen as a warning."

"Will that not just make him a martyr?" asked a thin old man. His face was covered in pale scars. "We need to deal with him purposefully. From what I understand he is quite the fighter. If his ideals were better, I would try to recruit him again."

There was a murmur around the table.

"As it is," the man continued, "he must be dealt with. But how?" He placed his fingertips together and furrowed his brow.

Ioseph leaned forward. "He needs to be humiliated. Disarm his strength of will and make him question --"

Anca flung herself at her brother. "YOU!"

Daran tried to hold her back. Her heel made contact with her brother's jaw, making a satisfying crack.

"Help me," Daran called.

Three others rushed forward. It took every one of them to tear her from her brother. The exhaustion from the fight didn't exist; her injuries didn't exist. All she cared about was hurting Ioseph.

"Hadn't you done enough to him!" Anca screamed at her brother. She was desperate to claw off his smug smile.

"We need to get him to Briton. He'll be able to get everything from these guys. We'll know everything by tomorrow," said one of the vampires struggling to keep her from her brother.

Anca through herself forward. He *had* to pay.

Daran grabbed her face with both hands. "When Briton's done with him, we'll hand him over to Trig."

Anca paused. She couldn't think of a better punishment for her brother. She knew what Trig was capable of. She could only imagine what Trig would do. *That anger will be turned on me when he finds out what he's done. When he finds what he is to me, that I knew.*

"Fine," said Anca.

"Here." Daran shoved a large duffel bag into her arms. "Go to that room and put anything that might be useful in here." He pointed to the farthest away room.

He was right: she needed to do something constructive. Pictures of flaming babies kept creeping in her head. She needed to be far away from her brother.

After a while, her anger had calmed enough that she was starting to feel the fight. Tired, Anca ran a finger along a row of books. She pulled a random selection off the shelf. *Blood Sacrifice, the Sacred Duty of the Brotherhood.* "Ugh." She dropped the book into a duffel bag with anything else she'd found that could be useful. When she'd filled the bag, she hiked it over her shoulder and made her way toward the exit.

They were just about done. The Ancients were long gone. However they'd removed them had left no trace. Tracking them had proved impossible. A couple dozen vampires were still mulling about looking for anything useful, watching the hostages. She gave a tired smile to Isobel and Nuru as she went into the exiting tunnel. They were both obviously getting tired. Nuru glanced up from his work. Isobel gave a halfhearted wave, holding her rifle low and loose.

Ioseph sprang forward, ripping the rifle from her grip.

"NO!" screamed Anca.

He fired at the explosives she had set behind the giant doors. The explosion knocked her backwards into the tunnel, her duffle bag slamming against the wall next to the entrance to the tunnel. The fire from the blast set off the other explosives they'd set and seared Anca's skin. A roar of fire and shifting rock nearly deafened her. She had a moment to fling an arm over her face before she was covered in falling rock. Then everything went dark.

She awoke to a scratching at the top of her head. She tried to bat it away but couldn't move her arm. Slowly, she began to feel. Everything hurt. She opened her eyes only to have dirt fall into them. She was trapped. Trying to push the ruble off herself she screamed in frustration.

"Anca?"

"Hello?" Twisting her head, she tried to look up toward the top of her head where the sound had come from. A faint blue light was shining on her.

"Thank Odin."

"Trig?"

A small insect looking robot crawled past her head. It had a small light shining on its front. "We're working on getting you and the others out. It is going to take us a while to move all the rubble. Most of the helpers that *could* make this go quicker are already on planes headed home."

"I guess I'll wait here then."

Laughter came from the small robot.

"How many?" she asked, suddenly serious.

There was a pause. "We honestly don't know. At least twenty."

She bit her lip to stop the tears. Twenty more dead, at least. At least her brother was finally dead. Anyone in that cavern wouldn't have survived the blast let alone the crushing ruble. She had been lucky herself, merely burned and buried. She thought about Isobel waving to her, giving Ioseph his opening to give them a last fuck you. Then she thought about Nuru and she dissolved into sobs.

It took two hours and fifty-seven minutes for them to reach Anca after she'd stopped sobbing. Counting had given her something to concentrate on. It took another twenty minutes to get her unburied enough for her to wriggle out. Her head hadn't been covered but her arms and hips had been pinned. Her left fibula was fractured. Most of her skin was burned. A tendon in her left thumb had been severed; they had to slice it open and reattach it as it had healed improperly.

When she stepped out of surgery Trig and Lita were waiting for her. "I'm fine." She raised her bandaged hand as proof. Her skin was a wreck. Her leg was casted under her pants giving her a pronounced limp. She'd nearly punched the two doctors that had rebroken her leg so they could reset it to heal straight. She would heal in a couple days or so. It could have been sooner, but they only had so much soil and many were hurt worse than her. She could wait a day before finding a pod. She needed to be with those that survived, remind herself that not everything was lost. It had been Lita's idea.

"You need to recover your heart first. That takes longer to heal," she'd said.

Lita stepped forward to pull her into a gentle embrace. "I'm so glad you're okay."

Anca turned to Trig. "How's Sarah? You never said…"

"She's alive," he said, answering the question she had dreaded to ask outright. "A boulder crushed her foot. Her ankle was severed. If they'd gotten to her sooner, maybe they would have been able to reattach it but…" He shrugged. "She's a couple rooms down. They're fitting her for prosthetics."

"I'm so sorry."

"She's alive. That's what matters." He crossed his arms, arcing an eyebrow. "Your brother?"

"About that." Her gaze dropped.

Lita looked from Trig to Anca in confusion. "What?"

"Ioseph was my brother."

"He was there? He's been alive this whole time?" She gripped her red hair in disbelief. She looked at Trig with an apprehensive look.

"Not anymore. Anca killed him." Trig nodded his approval.

"No, he killed himself. It sounded like us being able to infiltrate that place signed his death warrant, so he just did the job himself," said Anca. She wasn't ready to tell Trig everything yet.

"Wait, who signed his death warrant?" asked Trig.

"The people he works for. The people that ran that place. It was a tiny piece in their game. We didn't make a dent by destroying it. We're dealing with a much greater enemy than we thought."

"Just when I was starting to feel like celebrating, I find out we're in even deeper shit," said Lita.

CHAPTER 23

Anca ran around the Turkish facility taking in every face. She even hugged the werewolves. Every life spared had been a gift. She saw Etena and Goran share their first kiss, exhausted from helping the wounded. After a while Lita forced her to sit down and eat. Trig paced the courtyard, waiting for Sarah to come out.

Urian found them and gave Anca a silent hug. His embrace spoke volumes. When they broke apart, he took Lita's face in his hands and started asking her if she was alright. He seemed unconvinced by her repeated, 'I'm fine's'.

"You asked me to look after him. I thought the danger had passed…" Urian kept fidgeting.

"We all thought it was over," admitted Anca. *I should have just killed him centuries ago.*

Rage was easier. If she let herself think about Nuru for too long she would lose her ability to function. She concentrated on listening to Urian and Lita talk babies as intently as she could.

Sarah appeared in an archway nearly an hour later. Trig was at her side in a blink. "How's it feel?" He took her arm. "Didn't they offer you crutches?"

"Offered, yes." Sarah bit her lip in concentration.

"Stubborn," said Lita affectionately.

"Flirt," said Sarah.

"True." Lita smiled. Urian smirked next to her.

Sarah sat heavily in a chair next to Anca. "You look like shit."

"Thanks," said Anca.

"At least you're alive," said Sarah.

"True."

"What were we able to learn? I assume not *everything* burned," asked Sarah.

"Yeah, what *did* we learn?" Anca hadn't gotten any information for the past several hours, she had no idea what they knew. All the hostages had died in the explosion, so they couldn't get any information from them. She didn't even know if her duffle bag had made it. It was possible most of those books had burned. Only a few other vampires had hauled objects of interest out before her. They probably didn't have much to work with now.

"They were able to salvage most of the books from your bag, Anca but…" Trig shook his head. "That was the last they were able to salvage. Everything past the opening of the tunnel burned. Most of the books were on torture methods and history, not too much we can learn from it. There was one book about the Blood Brother's initiation process, so we're hopeful we can learn more about their organization as a whole from that. Sarah retrieved some financial files but --"

"But they got crushed with me. Plenty of it was torn to shreds. They can piece together some of it, but it will take time. It could shed some light on possible other headquarters. If there are more of these bastards, that's how we'll find out," said Sarah.

Urian nodded in agreement.

"There are more. I saw Ioseph talking with some woman that was clearly his boss. She said that facility was nothing. I don't think we even made a dent in whatever master plan they have," said Anca.

Sarah looked at her prosthetic foot. "What a shame."

Trig rubbed her shoulder. She leaned against him, eyes closed.

"What we do now is obvious then," Anca said.

Trig nodded at her knowingly. Lita gave her a puzzled look.

"Patch ourselves up, learn what we can, hunt down any threat, and teach any fucker who thinks they can mess with our family just how wrong they are," said Anca.

Trig nodded in agreement.

"Hell, yeah," said Sarah.

"You know we went into that fight thinking that was the end one way or another." Anca shook her head. "Turned out it was just the beginning."

FAMILY IS MORE THAN BLOOD

Made in the USA
Lexington, KY
25 March 2019